The Cache Code

by Kathy Sattem Rygg

The Cache Code | Kathy Sattem Rygg

ISBN: 978-1-5391740-9-7

1. Fiction 2. Fantasy 3. Middle Grade Fiction

Printed in the U.S.A.
First Edition, September 2016

ACKNOWLEDGMENTS

This third book in the Crystal Cache series did not come about easily. It was met with a number of obstacles, including the loss of half of the first draft of the manuscript. However, thanks to a network of people who supported, encouraged, and waited patiently, I was able to prevail and rewrite the missing chapters. Thank you to my trusted friends and fellow authors in The Fictionistas critique group: Dawn Ford, Shelly Nosbich, Mary Pleiss, Jennifer Rupprecht, and Alyssa Stieren. You are all so creative, talented, and your feedback is always spot on. Jennifer also serves as an amazing line editor! The cover designs are the creative talents of illustrator Zak Mitchell who continues to portray the essence of the characters. I'd also like to thank my publisher, Phillip Chipping with Knowonder, who supports my work with genuine enthusiasm. And of course I want to give my most heartfelt thanks to my sons, Jack and Peter, who are the reasons I started writing children's books in the first place.

Chapter One

Dylan dug through his dresser drawers looking for shorts and T-shirts. Everything he pulled out from underneath his winter clothes was wrinkled, but he didn't care. He stuffed them into the duffle bag his mom had laid out on the bed. He found his swim trunks—the same ones he had worn to Kari's birthday luau. They looked a little small. Maybe he had grown in the last three months? They'd still work though. It didn't matter what he wore to the beach as long as he could say he had been to the ocean.

Dylan was still shocked his parents had agreed to let him go to Tera's grandparents in California over New Year's Eve. EJ and Kari were going too, and Mr. Paine was driving them, which had been a huge selling point with Dylan's parents. How much trouble could four kids get into on a road trip when their chaperone was part of a top secret military operation?

Dylan threw some underwear in the bag, a few pairs of socks, and a hoodie. Hopefully he'd remember to pack his toothbrush before he left in the morning. Mr. Paine said they were leaving the next day at 0700 hours. Dylan planned to be on Tera's front porch at least ten minutes early, right after ringing EJ's doorbell to make sure he was on time.

He looked around his room to make sure he wasn't

missing anything, and his gaze landed on the Lego house he had built, which still held the earth crystal. After Kari decided to keep the wind crystal someone had anonymously given her on her birthday, he decided to give Mr. Paine the replica of the earth crystal that Tera had given him. He and Kari agreed they'd turn over the real crystals eventually, but neither of them was ready yet. Dylan was still afraid of 4E Labs getting the crystals, and he wanted to protect them—and Tera. Kari had been practicing her power and was able to both start and stop a wind storm. She still couldn't control wind that she hadn't created though. It drove her crazy. But knowing Kari, she'd probably figure out a way to do it. They didn't tell Tera or EJ they still had the real crystals—what they didn't know wouldn't hurt them, right?

Dylan carefully removed the roof of the Lego house and took out the earth crystal. He flipped his light switch off and sat on the edge of his bed, holding the rock in his palm. The green upside down triangle with the line through the center gave off a soft glow in the dark. The wind crystal's symbol was the exact opposite—a triangle pointing up with a line through the center. And according to the pictures of the other elements Mr. Lyman had shown him in the geology book, the fire symbol was an upright triangle with no line, and the water symbol was just a triangle pointing down.

He let out a long sigh thinking about the two remaining crystals. He and Mr. Lyman had scoured cache listings online, making a list of any cache in Colorado that might have anything to do with the word fire. It was a short list, and they hadn't found anything. Mr. Paine and his boss, Colonel Thornton, weren't convinced the last two crystals were even hidden in geocaches, but Dylan wasn't going to give up. He was still determined to find them before 4E Labs did. The company had been a dead end lately too. Jessica, the researcher who was undercover at 4E but working with Mr. Paine, still couldn't prove the company was behind Tera's kidnapping last spring. But Dylan believed they were. And they were still after the four elemental crystals that were thought to make up the creation stone. He just didn't know what they wanted it for.

The doorbell rang. He replaced the crystal and ran downstairs to answer it. He was surprised to see Mr. Lyman standing on the front porch.

"Hello, Dylan. I wanted to catch you before you left on your big trip tomorrow."

"Hi, Mr. Lyman. Come on in."

His neighbor took his time stepping inside. Dylan didn't know if the car accident they were in last summer had slowed him down permanently, or if it was from age. Mr. Lyman was old enough to be his grandpa.

Dylan's mom came into the entryway to greet him. "You're just in time for a slice of pie."

"I could smell it all the way down the street," Mr. Lyman said.

"Come sit down, and I'll get you some."

Dylan followed Mr. Lyman into the living room and sat down. "What did you want to see me about before I left?"

Mr. Lyman took a folded piece of paper out of his pocket. "I wanted to show you this." He handed it to Dylan. "It's a cache I found."

Dylan's heart beat sped up as he unfolded the paper.

"Is it a fire related cache? Is it close by?" He read the cache title and frowned—*Photo Finish*. There weren't any coordinates beside the title, just a big question mark. "So...what is this?"

"It's a puzzle cache. You have to solve the puzzle in order to find out the cache coordinates. I already solved it." Mr. Lyman smiled.

"Is this a new cache you just reviewed?" Dylan still couldn't figure out why Mr. Lyman thought he needed it. Especially before he left town.

"No, I didn't review this one. It's not local. It's actually on your route to California."

Dylan scanned the page. It had a bunch of text that looked like it talked about points of interest and historical locations along Interstate 70. "There isn't an encrypted code, so how am I supposed to figure out the coordinates?"

"That's part of the fun. You'll have to do a little research on puzzle caches. It'll give you something to do during the drive."

Dylan would have preferred a cache that might lead to a crystal, but solving a puzzle to get coordinates was a pretty cool idea. "Thanks. I'll start working on it tomorrow."

Mr. Lyman leaned forward in his seat. "I presume you still have the earth crystal?" he asked in a hushed voice.

Dylan felt his face redden. Kari was the only one who knew he had given Mr. Paine a fake crystal instead of the real one, but he trusted Mr. Lyman. "Yeah. It's safe and sound in my room."

"Good. And I take it you never recovered the wind

crystal after all your searching?"

Uh-oh. Dylan didn't want to lie, but Kari had sworn him to secrecy about that. He fluffed a pillow on the couch to avoid looking at Mr. Lyman. "Nope. We never found it." Technically that was true. He hadn't found it. Somebody had given it to Kari. They just didn't know who.

"That's a shame." Mr. Lyman coughed and cleared his throat. "You never know though. Maybe it'll turn up someday."

Dylan stole a glance at his neighbor. What did he mean by that? Did Mr. Lyman know Kari had the wind crystal? Was he the one who had given it to her? He was about to ask when his mom came into the living room, carrying two plates of pie.

"I even warmed it up for you," she said, handing Dylan and Mr. Lyman each a serving.

Mr. Lyman sat back in his seat and smiled. "Is this mince? My favorite. The holidays are never complete without it." He took a forkful. "This is delicious. It tastes just like Betty's used to—the perfect mix of sweet and hearty."

"Who do you think gave me the recipe?" Dylan's mom winked.

Dylan didn't remember meeting Mrs. Lyman. She died when he was really young. He took a bite of the pie and grimaced at the meaty taste—it was like dried up stew in pie crust. Why did older people like this stuff? He pushed the slice to the side of his plate and ate the vanilla ice cream instead.

His mom and Mr. Lyman chatted for awhile, so Dylan cleared their plates and brought them into the kitchen. He took the cache listing and smoothed it out on the counter.

He re-read the text on the first page and flipped it over. After the last paragraph there was a word search. Weird. Dylan had never seen a word search on a cache listing before. It must be part of the puzzle. The word search was ten letters across and ten letters down. Pretty simple. But where was the list of words to search for? He flipped the page back over and scanned the text. That's when he noticed some of the words were in italics—*cache, Colorado*, and *California*—all just in the first paragraph.

Dylan turned back to the word search, and within seconds he found the word *California* on the diagonal. He had figured out the puzzle! He grabbed a pen and made a list next to the word search of the rest of the italicized words from the front: *Colorado, cache, interstate, sights, Utah, Nevada, car, mileage*, and *map*. It took him only a few minutes to find and circle all the words. He'd always been good at word searches. But his pride quickly faded. What now? He still didn't have the cache coordinates.

Dylan went back into the living room with the paper. "Mr. Lyman, I solved part of the puzzle and found all the words in the word search, but I'm not sure what to do next."

"That didn't take long. Have you ever done a two-part word search before?"

"What do you mean by two-part?" Dylan scowled at his paper.

"You find the words but then are still *left* with another part to figure out." Mr. Lyman gave an encouraging nod.

Dylan stared at his neighbor for a minute. Why

had he emphasized the word *left*? He concentrated on the word search again. Then it hit him. He slapped his forehead with his hand. Duh! "I get it. You take the letters that are left after you've found all the words and put them together to form a sentence."

"Now you're on the right track." Mr. Lyman stood up.

"Where are you going?" Dylan didn't want him to leave in case he needed more help.

Mr. Lyman patted his stomach. "I need to go home before I eat another piece of pie and can't fit into my trousers anymore." He gave Dylan's shoulder a squeeze. "Have fun on your trip. Let me know if you find anything interesting in that cache."

Dylan's mom walked him to the door. Dylan turned his attention back to the word search, wrote down the remaining letters, and counted them—38 left. How was he supposed to figure out what 38 random letters spelled? That could take forever.

His mom came back into the living room. "Are you all packed?"

"I think so."

"Then you better get some sleep. You guys have an early start tomorrow." She kissed the top of Dylan's head.

"Night, Mom." He headed up to his room and got ready for bed. Before turning off his light, he spent a few more minutes with the word search letters. Where would he even start? He decided to separate them into vowels and consonants. But what next? There had to be some clue he was missing—some other part of the puzzle. He read the page of text again, but nothing stood out other than the italicized letters.

Black spots in his vision danced across the white page. Dylan rubbed his eyes and yawned. He turned off his light and laid his head back on the pillow with the paper resting on his chest. A soft green light radiated from inside his Lego house—the earth crystal. As he drifted to sleep, letters floated through his mind and arranged themselves like tiles on a Scrabble board. But none of them formed actual words—they were all nonsense. Except for one.

Fire.

Chapter Two

Dylan rang EJ's doorbell a second time and shifted his overstuffed duffle bag on his shoulder. He knew EJ wouldn't be ready on time. Mr. and Mrs. Doyle weren't morning people either. Most Saturday mornings during the summer when the other dads were mowing lawns, Mr. Doyle was just walking out to retrieve the newspaper from his driveway, wearing slippers and a robe.

After one more ring of the doorbell and a few loud knocks, EJ finally answered. He squinted against the morning light, his buzzed hair flattened against one side of his head in a lopsided mohawk. His black athletic pants pooled around his untied tennis shoes, and his grey hoodie had wet streaks across the arm—probably from where he had wiped his mouth on his sleeve.

Dylan grabbed the backpack dragging on the floor between EJ's feet. "What took you so long? We need to go."

"Dude, do you know how early it is? Even Hulk wouldn't get up. I had to push him off the end of my bed, and when I filled his dog food bowl he looked at me like I was crazy. Then he yawned and went back upstairs. I'm telling you, it's not fit for man or beast at this hour."

"Is this all you're bringing?" Dylan held up EJ's backpack.

"Oh man, I almost forgot." EJ went back into the

house and came out a minute later carrying a brown paper grocery bag.

"We're going to stop and eat on the road," Dylan said. "You don't need to bring that much food."

"It's not food. It's my clothes." EJ shut the door behind him.

"You packed your clothes in a paper bag? Then what's in the backpack?"

"*That's* got my food in it. And a bunch of baseball cards I need to organize. I figure it's a good way to pass the time on the road when I'm not sleeping."

Dylan shook his head, laughing to himself as they walked across the street to Tera's house. Her garage door opened, and Mr. Paine started loading bags into the back of his black Hummer.

"I was just wondering if you were going to make it on time." Mr. Paine wore khaki slacks and a navy sweater. Dylan had never seen him in grubby clothes. Even when Mr. Paine mowed the lawn he wore khaki shorts and a crisp white T-shirt.

Tera and Kari came out of the house pulling their suitcases, backpacks on their shoulders, and pillows tucked under their arms.

EJ tossed his paper bag in the car. "Geez, how long are you guys planning on staying in California, a year?"

"I'm just glad we don't have to share a room with you," Kari said. "Did you even bring a change of clothes?"

"I can wear the same pair of socks and underwear two days in a row then turn them inside out and get another two days out of them." EJ took a piece of licorice out of his backpack and stuck one end into his mouth.

Kari rolled her eyes. "You're such a Neanderthal."

EJ made ape noises and scratched his arm pits, then climbed into the third row bench seat of the Hummer. Dylan handed Mr. Paine his duffle bag and got into the car, sitting in one of the second row bucket seats. Kari sat next to him, and Tera sat in the front passenger's seat.

Mr. Paine closed the back hatch and got behind the wheel. "Everyone buckle up. Tera, you're my navigator. We're not stopping until lunch unless it's an emergency."

Tera pulled up a map on the car's dash navigation screen. Kari took a book out of her backpack, and EJ jammed in his ear buds then leaned his head back and closed his eyes. Dylan sat up in his seat and watched his neighborhood disappear as they drove off. He took the cache page Mr. Lyman had given him out of his backpack and stared at the list of letters again.

"What's that?" Tera asked, looking back at him.

"It's a puzzle cache located somewhere on our route to California. I've solved part of it, but I can't figure out what to do next. I think I'm supposed to put all these letters together and figure out what it says."

"Can I see it?"

Dylan handed Tera the paper. "They're the leftover letters after I found all the words in the word search."

"Are they in the order they were in on the word search, from left to right, top to bottom?"

"Yeah, they should be."

Tera studied the page a minute then took a pen and scribbled on the back of the paper. She looked at Dylan over her shoulder and smiled, handing him the paper.

He looked at what she wrote. *To find the coordinates check the source code*. Dylan stared at Tera, his mouth hanging open. "How did you do that?"

"I just took the letters you had written out and put them in order backwards."

Dylan continued to stare at her. Why hadn't he thought of that?

"My grandma does a lot of word searches, crossword puzzles, and Sudoku, so I've picked up a few tricks."

He turned his attention back to the sentence. "You don't happen to know what the source code is, do you?"

Tera shook her head. "You're lucky I got this far."

"It probably refers to the source code on the web site page." Mr. Paine glanced at Dylan in his rearview mirror. "Every web page is created using HTML code, and there are a lot of words and symbols in the code that don't show up on the finished page."

"You mean like hidden text?" Dylan asked.

Mr. Paine nodded. "Hidden text, numbers, and in this case, probably GPS coordinates."

"How do we get to the source code?"

"If you look at the web page on a computer, you can usually just right click anywhere on the page and select the 'view source' option."

Dylan did a quick mental inventory. He was pretty sure nobody in the car had a laptop or a tablet, and he didn't have Internet access on his phone. He might as well live in the dark ages.

"EJ, I need your phone for a second."

EJ didn't move or open his eyes.

Dylan tore a piece of paper from the notebook in his backpack, crumpled it into a ball, and threw it at EJ. It hit him square on the nose.

"Hey!" EJ bolted upright.

"I need your phone," Dylan said.

"Use your own phone."

"I need to look up something online and I don't have access. Come on, just hand it over." Dylan reached out his arm.

EJ sighed and unplugged his headphones then handed Dylan the phone. "Make it snappy, Fish."

Dylan opened the web browser and typed in the address printed on the cache page Mr. Lyman had given him. He tried highlighting the screen but didn't have a way to select the source code feature. "Aw, man. I need a computer to do this."

"There's one at my grandparent's house," Tera said.

"That'll be too late. The cache is located somewhere between here and there." Dylan gave the phone back to EJ and slumped in his seat.

Mr. Paine cleared his throat. "I might be able to help. My laptop is in the back. We could find a place for lunch that has Wi-Fi."

"I have an even better idea," Kari said, looking up from her book for the first time. "If EJ has Internet access, we can make his phone a hotspot and connect the laptop to the Internet that way." She gave a proud smile.

Dylan sat up again. "Awesome! Hey, EJ, I need your phone again."

EJ didn't respond.

Kari reached back and flicked EJ's outstretched leg with her fingers.

EJ scowled and yanked out his earbuds. "What now?"

"Give me your phone then reach in the back behind your seat and get Mr. Paine's laptop bag," Kari said.

"Please," she added slowly.

EJ grumbled but did as he was told, then popped open a can of Pringles and crunched loudly while he pouted in the back seat.

Kari gave Tera the laptop and worked on setting up EJ's phone to be a hotspot. "Um, EJ, if your parents ask you about an extra fifteen dollars on your phone bill, it's for the hotspot."

"What? I'm not paying that. Fish, you owe me fifteen bucks. Fork it over."

Dylan laughed. "I'll just take it off your bill. You owe me at least that much for all the soda and chips I've bought you from the Mini Mart."

"Okay, Tera. See if you can get online," Kari said.

Tera hit a few keys. "It worked!" She passed the laptop to Dylan.

"Thanks for letting me use this, Mr. Paine."

"Just don't tell anyone I let you use government property." Mr. Paine smiled at Dylan in the rearview mirror.

Dylan brought up the cache web site then selected the 'view source' setting. The computer screen flashed, bringing up line after line of strange text.

"There's a lot here. This might take me a few minutes." He scanned through it, trying to make sense of all the arrows, backslashes, and letter-number combinations.

Half-way down he saw something he didn't remember reading on the original page. It was a list of names—William McKinley, Benjamin Harrison, and John Tyler. He checked the cache printout again. The names weren't anywhere on the page, which meant they had to be a code.

"Hey, does anybody know who William McKinley, Benjamin Harrison, and John Tyler are?"

"Aren't they the members of that 70's band, The Beatles?" EJ yelled from the back seat. "My parents love their Jumping Jack Flash song."

Mr. Paine gave a loud laugh. "I think you're mixing up The Beatles with the Rolling Stones."

"They're all ancient to me," EJ said.

Kari leaned toward Dylan and looked at the computer screen. "Those are all names of U.S. presidents."

What did they have to do with GPS coordinates?

"They're listed out of order though." Kari pointed to the screen. "Tyler came first. He was the tenth president. Harrison was the twenty-third and McKinley was the twenty-fifth."

Dylan grinned. "Kari, I think you just found my coordinates."

Chapter Three

Dylan used the presidential numbers as coordinates and plugged them into his GPS. "It looks like the cache is right off the interstate, in Glenwood Springs."

"That's about 90 miles from here." Mr. Paine glanced back in his rearview mirror. "If we stop, I don't want to spend a lot of time looking for your cache. I'd like to stick to the schedule."

"It won't take long, I promise." Dylan was good at finding caches.

"Is this another potential crystal cache?" Mr. Paine didn't sound enthusiastic.

"No, it's a puzzle cache. Mr. Lyman gave it to me. I've never done one before."

"Another one of Mr. Lyman's?" Mr. Paine asked.

Dylan was willing to bet what Mr. Paine was thinking—all of Mr. Lyman's caches had helped lead to crystals. He doubted this one did though. It was just something fun Mr. Lyman thought he'd like to do on the trip.

Tera turned toward Dylan. "You'll have to look up some caches in California."

"I'm not spending my vacation geocaching," EJ said from the back seat.

"I'll go with you. Maybe there's one by the beach," Tera said.

Dylan smiled. He couldn't think of a better way to spend his vacation.

He settled into his seat and took out his phone. Playing games would be a good way to pass the time. He glanced out the window and noticed they were already driving through the mountains. The road curved around steep rock walls that towered just feet from the road's shoulder. In some spots black mesh netting covered the walls to keep falling rock from hitting cars on the road.

"Hey guys, look! The Big Horn sheep are out!" Kari scooted toward her window, looking up with her nose inches from the glass.

Dylan ducked, straining to see out the other side of the Hummer. He spotted one sheep perched half-way down the mountain, its thick, curled horns like two giant snail shells on either side of its head.

"My dad says the sheep come down the mountain during the winter months to find food because the tops are snow-covered," Kari said.

"Is there anything you don't know?" EJ pushed the back of her seat with his foot.

"It wouldn't hurt you to learn something once in a while," Kari shot back.

"I learn plenty. In fact, I'm going to learn how to surf in California. Right, Fish?"

"The only surfing I'll be doing is online." Dylan remembered when he tried to skateboard. His board had ended up wedged in the street's curb sewer, and he ended up with bloody knees and elbows.

"I want to try boogie boarding," Kari said. "It's just like surfing, but you don't have to stand up."

Dylan shook his head. "It doesn't matter what kind

of board I use. We don't mix."

"You could always try body surfing," Tera said. "No board required. It's easy and way more fun. I can show you how."

Now Dylan couldn't get to California fast enough.

He went back to his game, and a little while later he realized they were slowing down.

"Exit 116 for Glenwood Springs," Mr. Paine announced. "Where to, Dylan?"

Dylan fumbled for his GPS. "Right at the stop light and then the first left." He looked out the car windows for any areas that seemed like a geocaching spot. It looked like any other small town to him.

"According to your directions, we're heading for the Glenwood Hot Springs." Mr. Paine pulled into the parking lot of a large hotel. "Are you sure this is correct?"

Dylan remembered something he had read on the cache print out. "Yeah, I think it is. The cache web site talked about the Hot Springs being a big tourist attraction along I-70. It must be somewhere on the property. We'll have to get out and follow the GPS to the exact spot."

Mr. Paine turned off the engine. "I suppose it wouldn't hurt to stretch our legs."

Dylan climbed out of the Hummer and felt the inside of his nose frost over as soon as he breathed in the cold mountain air. Long wisps of cream-colored clouds spread across the blue-gray sky. In the distance, snow-capped mountains surrounded the valley.

EJ zipped his hoodie to his chin. "Let's get moving. It's freezing."

Dylan held the GPS out in front of him and followed the voice commands. "In 300 feet turn right." He led the group around the side of the hotel then came to a quick stop.

An Olympic-sized swimming pool ran the length of the hotel. Steam rose off the water, creating a haze that covered the top of the pool like a blanket. Through the mist, people swam, their dark heads bobbing out of the water.

"Whoa, those people are crazy," EJ said.

"It must be some sort of polar-bear club," Tera said. "Some people in California do this kind of thing—they swim in the ocean when the water's really cold."

A group of kids their age threw a ball back and forth in the water, laughing and yelling. They didn't act like they were freezing. Maybe the pool was heated?

"This is a hot spring," Mr. Paine said. "The water is naturally warm. That's why this place is a big tourist attraction and family vacation spot." He peered down over his aviator sunglasses. "Not a place for kids passing through to take a quick dip without paying." Mr. Paine pushed his glasses back up on his nose. "I'm going to find the restroom. Meet back at the car in fifteen."

As soon as Mr. Paine disappeared inside, EJ walked up to the edge of the pool and leaned over, swirling the water with his hand. "Dude, it feels like a hot tub!" He slid off his shoes, unzipped his hoodie, and rolled up his pants.

"Egan Doyle, what are you doing?" Kari scolded.

"I just want to stick my feet in." He stepped into the shallow end. "Ahhhh. You guys gotta try it."

Kari crossed her arms and tapped her foot.

"Come on, Fish, you don't want to miss this." EJ splashed water toward Dylan.

19

Dylan jumped backward. "No way. Tera's dad would kill us."

"We're not going to swim, just stick our toes in for a second." EJ grinned like a leprechaun.

"It can't hurt just to test it out." Tera kicked off her shoes, and Dylan did the same. Kari threw her arms up and let out a groan but then took her shoes off too.

"That's what I'm talking about," EJ said.

Dylan pushed up his pants and stepped into the pool. The water felt hot against his skin, like a splash from a boiling pot, but then quickly cooled to a comfortable temperature. He walked around in the knee-deep shallow end, wishing he could dive in. From the knees down his legs felt like they were wrapped in a blanket, but the rest of his body shivered.

"Bottoms up!" EJ tossed his hoodie to the side then dove under water, still wearing the rest of his clothes.

"What are you doing?" Kari scolded once EJ surfaced.

"Oh, it is so worth it. And I've got extra clothes in the car." He floated on his back, steam rising off his T-shirt.

EJ stood up in the shallow end, his arms outstretched. "Fish, where're you going? Aren't you getting in?"

"I need to find the cache so we can get back on the road." Dylan waited to see if EJ would get out, but he dove back underwater. "Figures." EJ never took geocaching seriously—he didn't take most things seriously.

Kari stepped out of the pool and grabbed four towels from a table nearby. Dylan dried off his legs, put his shoes and socks back on, and grabbed his GPS.

Tera and Kari were already dried off and waiting for

him.

"EJ you better be dried off and back at the car on time," Dylan said. "I'm not covering for you."

"I'll be ready in plenty of time." EJ spouted a mouthful of water. "You better not be late."

"We'll hurry." Dylan checked the GPS and led the girls away from the pool toward a grove of trees. They climbed a gradual hill that ended in a cement pad surrounded by a low stone wall. It overlooked the resort and hot springs pool.

"You have arrived at your destination," the GPS said.

"Dylan, look." Tera pointed at a sign posted on the wall. It said "Scenic Overlook" below an image of a camera. "Doesn't the cache title have something to do with photos?"

"Yeah. It's called Photo Finish." Dylan knelt and examined the metal sign. A screw at the top attached the sign to the wall, but the bottom wasn't secure. He moved the sign to the side so it pivoted where it was attached. Underneath, one of the rocks from the wall was missing.

Dylan reached in and pulled out a square tin that looked like an old metal lunch box. He sat back on his heels with the box on his legs and opened it.

"I wasn't expecting this. It's a bunch of pictures." He shuffled through them. They were all photos of people in front of the scenic overlook. "How did they get the photos printed?"

Tera knelt down beside him and reached her hand into the rock wall. She pulled out a funny looking camera. "They used this."

"What is that?" Dylan asked.

"It's a Polaroid camera," Kari said. "My parents used to have one. It develops the picture in minutes." She took a photo out of the box and turned it over. "The names and date of the people in the picture are listed on the back. That must be how you log that you found the cache instead of signing a slip of paper." She put the photos back and stood up. "Okay you two. Stand in front of the sign and I'll take your picture."

Tera quickly stood up, handed Kari the camera, and waited for Dylan. He got up and stood beside her. Should he put his arm around her like his dad always did to his mom in photos? He noticed Tera had her arms at her sides, so he did the same—pressing his hands against his legs.

"Smile!" Kari took the picture. The camera spit out a square piece of paper. Kari flapped it back and forth in her hand like a fan. "It'll just take a minute to develop."

Dylan bent over to pick up the box and accidentally dropped it, spilling the photos.

"Here, I'll help you." Tera leaned over, gathering a bunch. Then she slowly straightened, staring at one of the pictures.

"Tera, what's wrong?" Dylan asked. "You look like you just saw a ghost."

"I did." She turned the picture toward him. "It's a picture of Frank. My kidnapper."

Chapter Four

Dylan took the picture from Tera. She was right—dark hair, squinty eyes, burly build—it was definitely Frank. The trees and grass in the photo were bright green, so it must have been taken during summer. He turned the picture over and looked at the back. *Frank Caniglia*. There was no date beside it.

Tera's face matched the white stone on the wall, and her expression froze. Kari walked up and looked at the photo then put her arm around Tera, giving her a squeeze.

"Should we take the photo and show it to your dad?" she asked.

Tera slowly shook her head. "No. It won't do any good now."

Kari looked at Dylan. "But what if this cache has something to do with the crystals?"

He studied the photo again and frowned. "Like what? There's nothing here about fire or water or anything else. It has to be some crazy coincidence." Didn't it?

Kari paced in front of the rock wall. "What if it's not just a coincidence? What if there's more to the puzzle cache? Something that could lead us to another crystal?"

Dylan leaned against the wall. "Frank probably did tons of geocaching while he was looking for the earth crystal. Who knows? He could have checked every cache in Colorado trying to find the right one."

"Or…" Kari held up one finger like a teacher, "he could have just looked for caches that he thought might have something to do with the crystals, kind of like you've been doing."

"But I'm not sure Frank even knew about the other crystals. He only mentioned the earth crystal, besides—"

"Okay stop!" Tera said. "We could stand here all day trying to guess what Frank did and didn't know. Instead, let's focus on what we *do* know. He was looking for one of the crystals, and this is one of the places he tried. So, we can assume there must be something about this cache that made him stop here. I agree with Kari. There might be more to the puzzle."

Kari looked at Dylan and smirked.

He narrowed his eyes at her. "Don't you dare say 'I told you so.' Not yet anyway."

She gave him a sly smile. "We need to find out more about puzzle caches. See if there's any other hidden messages or codes we might be missing."

Tera held out the cache container toward Dylan. "We better get back. My dad will be waiting, and we can look all this puzzle stuff up in the car."

Dylan looked down at the photo of Frank in his hand. "You're sure you don't want to show this to your dad?"

"Positive."

He buried the photo of Frank in the cache.

"I don't want our photo in there…with him," Tera said.

"It's too cute to keep in a box anyway." Kari handed it to Dylan. "It'd be way better in a frame."

Dylan smiled when he saw the picture of him and

Tera. "Yeah, it's pretty good." He held it up for Tera. She gave a nod but still seemed disturbed by Frank's picture. Dylan slid their picture into his pocket and handed Tera the cache. She put it and the camera back behind the stone in the wall. The three of them headed back toward the hot springs. They walked single file, with Kari in the front and Dylan at the back. He thought about the puzzle cache and wondered whether or not there really was more to it. Then his thoughts drifted to Mr. Lyman—had he figured out a connection to the crystals? Is that why he had given Dylan this particular cache? He couldn't wait to get started—and he had the next twelve hours to figure it all out.

Mr. Paine and EJ were waiting for them by the car. EJ had changed clothes and was leaning against the Hummer, his ear buds back in his ears.

"Did you find the cache?" Mr. Paine asked.

Dylan, Tera, and Kari exchanged looks.

"Yep," Tera said. "Instead of a regular log book, you take a Polaroid to show you found it." She didn't look at Dylan or Kari.

Mr. Paine opened the passenger door for her. "Well I'm glad you found it. Now we can get back on the road and back on our schedule."

Dylan settled into his seat and turned on the laptop before Mr. Paine even started the car. He typed the words "puzzle cache" into the search engine and clicked on the listing from the geocache web site. It was a *lot* of information. He grabbed a pencil from his backpack and used the back of the cache paper to take notes.

Kari looked up from her book. "Wow. You're serious about this puzzle cache thing. Is there anything I can do to help?"

Tera turned around in her seat. "Yeah, I can help too."

Dylan didn't look up from the screen. "Thanks, guys. I'll let you know." He really wanted to figure this one out on his own.

There were way more puzzle caches than he realized—not just word searches and hidden messages in HTML code—but binary code conversions that used "1" and "0" to convert to letters, foreign languages, and even Braille. Dylan kept reading, his brain filling up with information he didn't even understand. But one thing stood out—puzzle caches were all about finding patterns, just like the italicized words for the word search and the list of U.S. Presidents.

He skimmed the web page until he got to the paragraph about anagrams—words that spell something new when the letters are rearranged. He remembered doing those in school. They took words like "tea" and changed it into "eat." It was kind of fun. But how was he supposed to know if there were any anagrams in this puzzle cache?

Dylan went back to the cache page online and started reading all the text again. Other than the italicized words he had used for the word search, nothing else stood out—no bolded words or strange letters or numbers. Not even a list of random words. He leaned back in his seat and ran his hands through his hair.

Tera turned and looked at him. "No luck?"

"It's like the worst brain teaser times a hundred."

"Want me to take a look?"

"Have at it." Dylan handed her the laptop and took

a granola bar out of his backpack. "I read that sometimes puzzle caches use anagrams so I was trying to find another coded word," he said before eating his snack in two big bites.

"I thought you found the puzzle cache," Mr. Paine said.

"We did, but..." Dylan wasn't sure what to say. He knew he couldn't tell Tera's dad about the photo of Frank.

"But there was a clue in the cache that there's more to the puzzle, so we're trying to solve it," Tera said.

Dylan saw the slight smile on her face. Her fingers tapped on the keyboard, and he leaned forward to watch. She brought up the source code page where he had found the president names, and she scrolled through it.

"Did you notice these letters that are in a different font color?" Tera pointed to a bright green capital "A" on the screen.

Dylan shrugged. "I don't know. Not really. Why? Do you think it means something?"

"I'm not sure yet. Five lines down there's another green letter—a lowercase 'c.' And here's a lowercase 't' below that."

"That spells 'Act.' Are there any more?" Dylan sat so far forward it stretched his seatbelt tight across his chest, and he wished he could take it off and get closer to Tera for a better look.

She scrolled down the page. "Here's another lowercase 'a' and a lowercase 's.'" She pointed each one out to Dylan. "And the last paragraph has three—an 'o', 'n', and an 'e.'"

"So what does all of that spell out?" Dylan should have been writing it all down.

"It spells 'Act as one,'" Kari said.

Dylan hadn't noticed that she had closed her book and was taking notes. He sat back in his seat. "'Act as one?' What's it supposed to mean?" He wondered if it might have something to do with the crystals—that you needed all of them together to make the creation stone—but he didn't want to say it in front of Mr. Paine.

"I don't know, but that's what it spells." Kari held up her notebook where she had written all the letters down.

"Why don't we try doing the anagram thing with it?" Tera suggested. "Everyone come up with as many different words as you can using the phrase 'Act as one.'"

Dylan borrowed a piece of paper from Kari's notebook and wrote the phrase in large letters at the top. Then he made three columns—one for two letter words, one for three letter words and another for four letter words, just like his teacher had showed him in school.

NO	CAT	CASE
ON	SAT	TONE
TO	TOE	
AT	NOT	
AN	TEA	

When he couldn't come up with any more words, he studied his list. Other than twelve random words, he didn't see anything they had in common—no pattern.

Tera turned around as far as she could in her seat.

"Okay, let's see what everyone has. Kari, why don't you read your list first and then we can add ours to it."

"I came up with twenty-three words." Kari started reading her list.

Dylan couldn't believe how many he had missed—and easy ones too, like "net," "ten," "ace," "nose," "stone," and "neat." Good thing he didn't read his list first. That would have been embarrassing.

"Okay, Dylan how about you?" Tera asked when Kari was done.

"Uh, I think Kari had all the same ones I did." He laid his arm across his paper so they couldn't see his puny list.

"You forgot a really obvious one." Everyone turned to look at EJ, who yawned and stretched in the back seat. "Write this one down, Kari. S-C..." Kari scribbled in her notebook. "...A-T. Scat. You know, animal dung."

Kari groaned and flung her pencil at EJ. He laughed, tossing it back.

Tera looked at her sheet. "The only one I had that Kari didn't was 'Sacatone.'"

Dylan thought she had to have used the online dictionary. "What's a sacatone?"

"It's a place outside of San Diego. I've seen signs for it on the way to my grandparents' house, right Dad?"

Mr. Paine nodded. "The Sacatone Overlook is about seventy miles east of San Diego."

Tera whipped around in her seat and gaped at Dylan.

His mouth dropped open—another overlook like the one at Glenwood Springs? It had to be a new part of the puzzle cache! He looked at Kari, whose expression was just as shocked.

"Did you say Sacatone is an *overlook*?" she asked Mr. Paine.

"It's just off Sacatone Springs Road. The area is a desert but scenic, and it's known for some pretty impressive granite formations."

Dylan's heart almost thumped out of his chest. There were *rocks* at the Sacatone Overlook too?

Tera turned toward her dad. "If it's east of San Diego, can we go there on our way into town?"

"Not today. We're already behind schedule. Maybe on the way back."

Dylan knew he couldn't wait that long and wondered if Tera was thinking the same thing he was—they had to get to Sacatone Overlook and find the rest of the puzzle cache—and anything else that might be hidden there.

Chapter Five

Dylan rolled onto his side, wrapping up in the warm blanket like a burrito. The smell of coffee and maple syrup met his nose, making his stomach rumble. When they'd arrived in San Diego late last night, Tera's grandmother had promised to make them homemade pancakes in the morning. Dylan smiled at the thought, and then opened his eyes—two inches from his face was EJ's sleeping body, a string of drool hanging from the corner of EJ's mouth.

Dylan got out of bed and shuffled to the window. It had been too dark to see much when they got in, but now he noticed the towering palm trees that lined the street like umbrellas. The grass was a summer green and flowers were in full bloom. In the distance the light blue sky turned darker blue at the horizon—the ocean!

EJ rustled and sat up, rubbing his eyes. "Oh man, something smells good. I hope there's bacon to go with the pancakes. We're going to need it if we're hitting the waves today."

Dylan had wanted to go to the Sacatone Overlook, but everyone else had agreed to spend their first day in California at the beach. He wanted to see the ocean too, but he couldn't stop thinking about the last part of the puzzle cache. He had heard Mr. Paine tell Tera's grandparents he had meetings to attend the next few days at the base. Dylan figured this meant he wouldn't be able to take them to Sacatone, so he'd have to figure out a way to get there on his own. The overlook was about an hour away from San Diego. A taxi would be too expensive, but he might be able to take a bus—he'd have to look into that.

EJ fished his swim trunks out of his grocery bag and went into the bathroom. Dylan changed into his swim trunks and then went into the kitchen for breakfast. Everyone else was already up.

"Good morning, Dylan." Tera's grandmother stood in front of the stove. She wore a red apron smeared with flour and held a spatula in her hand.

"Good morning, Mrs. Paine." Dylan slid into an empty chair at the table.

"Please, call me Gloria. I trust you slept well?" She placed a tall glass of orange juice in front of Dylan. "Freshly squeezed from oranges right off our tree."

"Thanks. Yeah, I slept great. EJ should be out in a minute too." He took a sip of juice. It was like sucking on a sweet orange wedge.

Tera and Kari were already eating pancakes. They both wore jean shorts and white tank tops and had the ends of their bright swimsuits tied behind their necks. Tera's dad and grandfather were sitting on the deck drinking coffee, both hidden behind sections of the morning paper.

EJ walked into the kitchen and grabbed a piece of bacon out of the skillet before plunking down at the table. "I can't wait to hit the beach and get my hands on a surfboard. Somebody has to go with me. Who's in?"

Kari finished her pancakes and slid her plate forward. "I might try it. Balancing on a surfboard could be a good skill for soccer."

"Tera? Fish? What about you guys?" EJ leaned back in his chair as Gloria placed plates stacked with pancakes in front of him and Dylan.

"I will if Dylan will, but I'm good with just hanging out too." Tera took a long sip of juice and looked at Dylan over the rim of her glass.

As he drizzled syrup over his pancakes, Dylan tried to decide how to answer. He knew he wouldn't be good at surfing, but he didn't want to let his friends down—especially Tera. And even though she said she'd do what he wanted, he knew she wanted to surf too.

"Okay. I'm in."

"Sweet! You won't be sorry." EJ took the syrup and drowned his pancakes.

After breakfast, Kari and Tera did the dishes while Gloria made sandwiches and packed a cooler. Dylan and EJ loaded her minivan with everyone's towels and beach bags.

Tera's dad was staying behind to work. "Listen to Gloria and Harold and don't go out too far in the ocean." He waved them off from the driveway as they left.

It was only a twenty minute drive to the ocean, and Dylan's nerves grew the closer they got. They parked along the street and walked down a narrow pathway to the public beach. There were only a few families who had claimed spots and some joggers running along the coast line. They picked an open spot, and Harold staked their umbrella in the sand.

"I see the surf rental shop," EJ said. "Let's go."

"Don't you kids want to take a lesson first?" Harold settled into his foldout lounge chair.

"Nah. How hard can it be? Besides, Tera's done it before. She can give us a few pointers."

Dylan glanced at the water. The waves rolling in didn't look much taller than him. How bad could it be?

They followed EJ to a wooden hut not far down the beach. A hand-painted sign on a piece of wood read "Board rental: $5."

"Five bucks. That's not so bad." EJ walked up to the guy in the hut who had a pony tail. "We need four surfboards for the day."

"Sure thing. That'll be ninety-six dollars."

"What? The sign says five bucks. It should only be twenty dollars." EJ backed up and pointed at the wooden sign.

"It's five bucks for one hour. Twenty-four for the whole day." The guy yawned.

EJ shook his head and mumbled something about a rip-off. Then he slapped a twenty dollar bill onto the wooden ledge in the hut window. "Fine. We'll have four boards for one hour."

The guy threw the money into a jar. "Have you ever surfed before?"

"No," EJ said.

"Trust me. An hour will be plenty of time." He walked out of the hut and handed them each a surfboard from a rack.

Dylan's board was white with blue waves on top. It was a little taller than him, and lighter than it looked.

"Here's your thirty second lesson," the guy said. "First, secure the leash to your leg so you don't lose the board." He held up a long piece of thick black Velcro on a string attached to EJ's board. "Next put your boards on the ground and lie on it stomach down with half your weight in front and half in back. Practice popping up a bunch of times, like this." He took EJ's board and laid down on it. "Pretend like you're doing a push-up, and pop into a crouching position." He jumped onto his feet, bending low like a sumo wrestler with one foot in front of the other. "Ride a few waves in on your stomach first to get the feel. Make sure you paddle one arm at a time to keep your board straight, and stay ahead of the wall of whitewater. Oh, and whatever you do, don't look at your feet, otherwise you'll fall every time. Guaranteed. Any questions?"

Dylan had a hundred questions but didn't have a chance to ask any of them—everyone else grabbed their surfboards and headed toward the water. He only got in a few practice pop-ups, and then his friends were ready to paddle out. He took his time securing the leash to his leg, hoping to buy a few extra minutes.

"Are you coming?" Tera waited for him a few feet in the water.

Dylan sucked in a deep breath of salty ocean air. "Please just don't let me drown," he whispered, and then walked into the water. A shock of cold wrapped around his ankles like he had just stepped in a bowl of ice cubes. "It's freezing!" Now he knew why surfers wore wet suits. He'd give anything to be back in the hot springs.

"Yeah, the ocean's pretty chilly in the winter. You'll get used to it though." Tera lay down on her board once Dylan reached her. They paddled out into deeper water where Kari and EJ waited, then turned so they faced the beach. Within minutes a wave rolled toward them.

"Start paddling!" EJ yelled.

Dylan's arms turned like a windmill as he tried to stay ahead of the wave. Suddenly, he didn't need to paddle anymore—the wave carried him. He held on to the sides of the board, thrilled that he had caught it on the first try and too stunned to try and stand up. It only took seconds for him to reach the shore.

"Woo hoo!" He hopped off and turned to see who else made it. He was the only one.

"Way to go, Dylan!" Tera waved and Kari gave him a thumbs up. EJ's head popped out of the water.

Dylan paddled back out. "What happened?"

"We were too slow, and EJ wiped out," Kari said.

EJ shook the water off his head. "I tried standing up, and I had it for a second."

They pointed their boards toward the beach again and waited for another wave. As one rolled in, they all started paddling. Tera was to Dylan's right and EJ was to his left. Dylan felt his board surge forward as the wave embraced it, and without thinking, he pushed himself into the pop-up position, crouching so low his bottom almost touched the board. He was doing it—he was surfing!

With a quick glance in each direction, he saw Tera try to stand up and then wipe out, and EJ wiped out right after her. When he reached shallow water, Dylan hopped off his board. Everyone else looked like wet zombies, dragging their boards through the water.

"Dude, you were awesome! How did you do that?" EJ gave Dylan a high-five.

"I don't know. I was barely standing up though."

"It still counts."

Tera squeezed water out of her pony tail. "I thought you said you were bad at this kind of thing? I've surfed before, but you'd never know it today."

"I think this gives a whole new meaning to your name, Fish." EJ slapped him on the back. "Come on, maybe you can give me some pointers."

Dylan's confidence soared as he looked at his friends' smiling faces. He had never been better than EJ at sports. Even Kari was always more athletic. Who knew he'd be better than them at surfing? And they were all proud of him—EJ didn't even seem jealous.

Dylan got back on his board and paddled out again, anxious to join his three best friends. He was glad they had decided to come to the ocean today and forgot all about geocaching—almost.

Before they knew it, their hour was up, and they dragged their boards onto the beach and turned them in at the rental hut. Tera's grandparents waved them over where they had snacks waiting.

"Looks like you guys got the hang of it." Harold sat in a low fold-out beach chair with dark sunglasses clipped over his regular glasses. He wore a yellow and blue Hawaiian shirt and a wide floppy hat. "Makes me want to have a go at it again."

Gloria laughed. "You had your day in the sun. Just stick to your rocks."

Dylan perked up. "What kind of rocks?"

"Oh, she's just talking about my fossil collection." Harold waved it off.

"I didn't know you had a fossil collection, Grandpa."

"Haven't touched it in years."

With the confidence he got from surfing still running

through him, Dylan decided to make a bold move. "Mr. Paine, how would you like to go on a rock expedition tomorrow?"

The corners of Harold's mouth turned up. "What do you have in mind, son?"

"Do you know where Sacatone Springs is?" Dylan glanced at Tera, who smiled and nodded her encouragement.

"That's about seventy-five miles from here," Harold said.

"If you're willing to drive, I can make it worth your time." Dylan's heart thumped as he waited for a reply.

Harold paused for what seemed like forever before responding. "Count me in."

Chapter Six

When Dylan walked into the kitchen the next morning, he was surprised nobody else was up. The coffee pot hadn't even started yet. Then he realized why — the digital clock read 5:58. He glanced at his watch — 6:58. He had totally forgotten about the hour time difference between Colorado and California. He opened the fridge and took out the pitcher of orange juice. When he closed the door he jumped. Tera stood behind it in her pink and purple plaid pajama pants and purple T-shirt, her ponytail bunched on one side. Dylan ran a hand through his hair, hoping it wasn't sticking up too much.

"Sorry, didn't mean to scare you. I didn't realize anyone else was up." The coffee pot clicked and started dripping into the pot.

Dylan searched the cabinets for two glasses. "The time change messed up my sleep." Plus he was so excited to go to the Sacatone Overlook, he couldn't sleep anyway.

"Glasses are in the cabinet above the sink." Tera slid into a kitchen chair. "I can't stop thinking about our trip today."

Dylan smiled at their similar thoughts.

"At least I'm not worried anymore about whether or not I'm a catalyst for all four crystals."

"You're not?" Dylan had never heard her say that

before.

"Nope. After finding out Kari can control the wind crystal, I'm convinced there are four different catalysts. I'm just not sure we'll ever know who the other two are."

"Maybe that's a good thing. If we don't know, then 4E Labs probably doesn't either. I just want to find all four crystals so we know they're safe." *And that Tera is too,* Dylan thought.

Harold and Gloria came into the kitchen, followed by Mr. Paine. "Look at these two early birds," Gloria said. "I better get some eggs cooking."

Kari joined them a few minutes later. Dylan thought he was going to have to wake EJ up, but as soon as Gloria started sizzling bacon, EJ shuffled out.

By eight o'clock Dylan and his friends were in the minivan, ready to go to Sacatone. Only Harold was going with them—Gloria was going grocery shopping (EJ had eaten all the bacon) and Mr. Paine was working.

"We're not spending the whole day geocaching, right Fish? I want to go see the Army ships Harold talked about." EJ pulled a cold piece of bacon out of his pocket and gnawed at it. Kari stuck out her tongue and made gagging noises.

"No, we're just going to find this one cache and then we can come back and see the Navy ships." Dylan unfolded the directions to the Sacatone Overlook he had printed off and handed them to Harold. "Here, just in case you need them."

"Thank you. I know the general area, but I've never been to the Overlook. What exactly is it you're after?"

"I'm not sure." Dylan smiled. That was one of the best things about geocaching—not knowing what you might find. "There could be anything in a geocache. Coins, photos, rocks..." He glanced at Tera who was reading a fashion magazine. One corner of her mouth turned up in a smile.

"Maybe this will be your lucky day," Harold said.

Dylan sure hoped so.

It seemed like it didn't take long before they were turning off the Interstate and winding through a desert. Dusty mountains stacked against the horizon, and clumps of green shrubs spotted the sandy landscape. Dylan read the directions for Harold, instructing him when to turn.

"This is the McCain Valley. It's a wildlife management and rec area." Harold slowed the car down. It was kicking up a lot of dust.

"Who'd want to camp here?" EJ asked. "No trees, no streams. Just a bunch of big, ugly rocks."

"I bet sunsets in the desert are pretty," Kari said. "And you wouldn't have to worry about bears."

"Nope, just snakes and coyotes." Harold pulled off the road into a small parking area. "But the snakes don't come out as much in the winter."

"That's probably because they're staying away from the coyotes," EJ mumbled.

They all got out of the minivan and headed up a steep gravel path. Tera held on to her grandfather's arm. Dylan decided to walk behind them in case Harold slipped. The path eventually leveled out and opened onto a flat overlook surrounded by a low, rock wall made from similar white boulders they saw at the entrance. Layers of tan mountains filled the sky as far as they could see. They weren't the Rocky Mountains of Colorado, but they were still impressive.

Harold inhaled a loud breath. "Ah. The Carrizo Gorge. Beautiful, isn't it?"

EJ cupped his hands around his mouth and yelled, "Helloooo!" But it didn't echo.

Kari shook her head. "We're not at the Grand Canyon, genius."

"It's a desert with a bunch of rocks. Same thing." He turned toward Dylan. "Okay, Fish. Where should we start looking?" EJ threw a few small rocks off the edge of the overlook.

"The last one was in a wall, so I guess we start looking for a loose stone." Dylan walked up to the wall. As soon as he saw how far down the ground was, his stomach plummeted. His vision blurred for a second, so he bent over and took deep breaths. Too bad he didn't have a paper bag to breathe into, as his first-aid instructions on fainting suggested.

"Are you okay?" Tera leaned over beside him.

"Yeah. I just got light-headed for a second. Too close to the edge."

"Come over here." Tera helped him up and led him to a far corner of the overlook away from the wall.

Dylan turned so his back was to the wall and to Tera. He didn't want her to see how freaked out he was. "I'm fine, I'll just—" He stared at a dark opening in the side of a small hill down from the overlook. It looked like…

"Is that a *mine*?" Tera grabbed Dylan's arm like she might faint and needed support.

Dylan hoped she didn't want to go down there and find out. Why did the crystals and mines always seem to go together? "Let's help the others look for the cache." He tried to make his voice sound positive despite the rock-like lump in his throat. Harold walked up to them before he could lure Tera away.

"Ah, that must be one of the active mines. Lots of spessartite in there, I imagine."

"Lots of what?" Dylan hadn't heard of that type of rock before.

"Spessartite. It looks like garnet—a deep red color."

From the bright look on Harold's face, Dylan was afraid *he* might want to go check out the mine.

Kari walked up to the group. "EJ and I did a quick check of all the stones along the wall. Nothing."

Dylan glanced around the overlook. If the cache wasn't in the wall, then where was it? His gaze landed back on the mine opening and dread swallowed him. It was the only other place that made sense. He doubted the cache would be hidden in the middle of this huge desert—the listing didn't give any specific coordinates to help find it. "Sacatone" was the only clue, and the only things in Sacatone were the overlook and that mine.

"Come on. I think I know where it might be." He led the group back down the path and stopped in front of the small opening. He pulled Tera aside. "You don't have to go in there."

She gave him a reassuring smile. "It's okay. I want to."

Harold took a couple steps inside. "I don't suppose anyone has a flashlight?"

EJ took out his cell phone and turned on his flashlight app, lighting up the inside of the mine with a bright white glow. "Cool. Is this what the inside of the mine at Dove Mountain looked like too?"

Dylan slugged EJ in the shoulder. Didn't he know

better than to say something like that in front of Tera? He ignored the question and walked farther in, but he couldn't help notice the inside was pretty similar to Dove Mountain. The tunnel was narrow and the ceiling low. But the walls were different—instead of dark, ragged rock, this rock was closer to the color of chalk. It was also speckled with dark spots—a few places even looked like they sparkled in the light from EJ's phone.

Kari ran her hand along the wall. "They look like rubies."

"It's spessartite." Dylan realized he must sound like a know-it-all. "Right, Harold?"

"It sure is." Harold's voice sounded far away and dreamy as he picked at a section of wall with his finger. Little bits of rock and dust fell to the ground. He took out a pocket knife and worked at chipping out a small section.

"Sweet. I want one too." EJ picked up a stone off the ground and hammered the wall. The
sound echoed throughout the mine.

"Are you sure it's okay to do that?" Dylan looked back toward the mine entrance as if someone would hear EJ's hammering.

"There weren't any "no trespassing" signs posted," Harold said.

Kari picked up a rock and started helping EJ on his claim. "Find your own spot," he said.

"If we work together, we can get a bigger chunk."

Harold, EJ, and Kari's hammering, chipping, and banging took on a steady rhythm that filled the small cavern. Dylan and Tera stood back in silence. He couldn't keep the thoughts of what happened in Dove Mountain out of his mind. The hammering grew louder, reminding him of the roar of the earthquake he and Tera had barely escaped.

In the dim backlight of the cell phone Tera's eyes looked dark and glossy. She was probably having similar thoughts—only for her they were more like nightmares. Without thinking, Dylan reached out his arm and took her hand. She clasped it tight. He gently squeezed it back.

"Ha, I got it!" The hammering stopped as Harold turned to show off his prize. A tennis ball size piece of white rock lay in his palm. Several chunks of dark red stone clumped in the middle of it. "You were right, Dylan. This trip was worth my time. Any luck finding what you were looking for?"

Dylan really didn't care about the puzzle cache anymore. He just wanted to get out of there. "No, but that's okay. We can go."

"I don't think so." The deep voice came from behind them. A man's figure filled the mine entrance. "No one's going anywhere yet."

Chapter Seven

At the sight of the stranger, Dylan gasped and inhaled such a large gulp of air, he sputtered and choked, launching into a coughing fit.

"I don't believe you folks have permission to be in my mine," the man said.

Harold walked toward him. "I apologize, mister…"

"Gordon. Chuck Gordon. And you are…?"

"Harold Paine." Tera's grandfather held out his hand, which Mr. Gordon accepted. "This is my granddaughter and her friends. It's our first time here, so we weren't aware we were trespassing. There aren't any signs posted."

The looming figure stood silent for several seconds. "I never used to have to worry about much foot traffic around here, but ever since the area became a campground, I've had to chase out my fair share of undesirables. I should probably post some signage."

Dylan wondered if Frank had been one of the undesirables. He heard Tera's breathing behind him and wondered if she thought the same thing.

"I'm a bit of a rock collector and helped myself to a small piece." Harold showed Mr. Gordon his claim. "I'm happy to pay you for it."

Mr. Gordon let out a booming laugh that echoed throughout the tunnel. "Not necessary. As you can see, there's plenty of the stuff here. Say, how would you like to see a piece ten times that big?"

Dylan's nerves settled at the man's friendly offer.

Harold looked at the kids. "I think we'd like that. What d'ya say?"

The kids nodded and filed out of the mine. Dylan was glad to have any excuse to get out of there.

Kari walked up beside him. "What about the cache? We didn't find anything."

"Without exact coordinates, it'd be impossible to find it." He shrugged. "Let's just go."

Kari pursed her lips but didn't say anything else. Dylan was glad she let it go.

An old, forest-green pick-up truck, with patches of rust around each wheel well, was parked next to their minivan. Mr. Gordon opened the driver side door, which let out a loud creak, and climbed in. "Follow me about a half mile up the road. My place is on the right."

Harold drove them a short way to a small single-story house with a roof that slanted down toward the front like a shed. Faded white paint peeled from the boards, and gaping holes covered the screen on the front door.

EJ leaned in toward Dylan. "I'll bet you a million bucks there's a dead body in there," he whispered.

"Just one?" Dylan said. The boys chuckled as they got out of the car and followed Harold and Mr. Gordon into the house.

Dylan stopped laughing the second he stepped inside. The small family room reminded him of the museum at Dove Mountain. Glass display cases filled with rocks lined the walls and dozens of framed photos

47

hung above them. A long, fancy dining room table sat in the middle of the room, displaying a rock buffet. Most were the same type they had found in the mine—light grey to white in color with clumps of dark red stones embedded on one side. The largest rock was the size of a grapefruit and almost entirely made of the red stones.

"This is quite a collection." Harold walked around the table, picking up each one and squinting at it through his thick eyeglasses.

Mr. Gordon puffed out his chest. "Mined every single one myself."

Dylan left the table to look in the display cases. Most of the rocks under glass were ordinary—dark colored stones in odd shapes and sizes. He had no idea what any of them were. Mr. Lyman would have loved it, and Dylan was pretty sure his neighbor would be able to identify every single one.

The last display in the corner by the kitchen caught Dylan's eye. This one was full of gemstones—deep colored rocks that were polished and perfected. Mr. Gordon had them lined up in a single row. Each one had a black and white printed label below it: *Garnet, Amethyst, Aquamarine, Emerald*.

"They're all the birthstones." Tera had joined him at the display case. "But April is missing. There's no diamond."

Dylan glanced at her and noticed the diamond earrings her dad had given her for her birthday. Last April.

"There used to be a diamond in there, but I sold it. Needed some extra cash." Mr. Gordon's cheeks turned red and he stared at the floor. Dylan had no idea how this guy could live off his rock mining.

"In addition to the money, the seller gave me something in exchange. I wasn't sure how to classify it, so I haven't put it out yet. Here, I'll show it to you." Mr. Gordon hurried out of the room. A minute later he came back, his right fist clenched. Everyone gathered around him. He paused for effect, like a magician about to perform a trick, and then he opened his gorilla-sized palm.

Dylan's jaw dropped like a skeleton when he saw the stone in Mr. Gordon's hand—a clear crystal the size of a golf ball with a reddish-orange mark in the center that looked like a triangle. He blinked several times to make sure he wasn't seeing things. Could it actually be what he thought it was? Here, in this mining guy's old run-down house? He leaned in closer. There was no way it was a coincidence. It had to be the fire crystal.

Dylan looked at his friends' faces, and their bug eyes and open mouths confirmed it. Harold was the only one who didn't look shocked. He let out a low whistle.

Mr. Gordon smiled. "I thought it might have come from the mine since the middle has a similar color as the spessartite, but I've never seen it in anything this clear before."

"It's quartz," Dylan breathed. "Who gave it to you?"

"I dunno. He was a young fella, said he found it by the overlook."

So somebody else had already found the cache, Dylan thought. And obviously the guy didn't know what the crystal was. "Can I see it?"

Mr. Gordon gave Dylan the crystal. Its smooth surface felt warm, probably from Mr. Gordon holding it.

"Can I try?" Tera whispered.

Dylan knew she wanted to test it to see if she was a catalyst. He hesitated but handed it to her. She had a right to find out.

Tera took the crystal in one hand and placed her other hand over it, closing her eyes. She waited several seconds then opened them again and shook her head.

Kari held out her hand. "Let me try." Tera passed her the rock. Kari closed her fist around it and her eyes lit up. "It's really warm."

"Yeah, it was for me too," Dylan said, and Tera nodded.

Kari looked disappointed but held the crystal out to Dylan.

"Hey, what about me?" EJ asked.

Kari scowled. "What about you?"

"Don't I get to hold it?"

Kari rolled her eyes and dropped the crystal into EJ's hand. He clasped it between his palms and held them in front of his face like he was praying. "Ommmmmm."

"Quit kidding around." Kari grabbed his arm.

"I'm not done!" EJ jerked away. "Dude, this thing *is* warm."

"We know. Now give it back to Dylan." Kari reached for EJ again.

"Calm down and quit trying to tackle me!" EJ said.

Kari tried prying open EJ's hands, but he turned his back on her. She wrapped her arms around him, trying to get to the crystal.

"Ouch!" EJ dropped the rock, and it landed on the floor with a thud. "What'd you do that for?" He rubbed his hands, wincing in pain.

"Oh relax. I barely touched you." Kari picked up the rock and handed it back to Mr. Gordon, who was scowling at them.

Harold cleared his throat several times. "That's enough horsing around, kids. I think perhaps we should be going now."

None of them moved. There was no way Dylan was leaving without the fire crystal. But what was he supposed to do? He didn't have any money to buy it from Mr. Gordon, and he didn't have anything to trade him either. Dylan stared at the crystal in the large man's hand. This was even worse than the time he found a lost puppy in his yard. He took care of it, named the dog George because it was curious and got into everything, and his parents even agreed he could keep it. Then the owners showed up three days later. Dylan had never gotten over it.

"Mr. Gordon?" Kari's voice broke Dylan's thoughts. "It sounds like the guy who found that rock took it out of a geocache. They're special hidden containers people are supposed to find. That's actually what we were looking for when we got sidetracked in your mine."

"Yeah, we were really hoping to find the cache," Dylan added.

Mr. Gordon closed his fist around the crystal like a child protecting his prize. "I'm sorry you came all this way for nothing."

Dylan's jaw tightened. The man was being stubborn.

"Hang on. I'll be right back." EJ jogged out of the house toward the minivan.

"What's he doing?" Tera asked. Dylan shrugged.

EJ came back into the house, carrying his backpack.

He reached in and pulled out a card wrapped in plastic. "Mr. Gordon, do you like the Boston Red Sox? This is my 2009 Dennis the 'Oil Can' Boyd baseball card. It's worth about fifty bucks. I'll give it to you for that rock."

Dylan gasped. He knew EJ's baseball card collection was his most prized possession. He couldn't believe he was willing to trade a card worth that much.

"Hold on, surely you're not going to make this boy give up something of such value. Your rock isn't worth that much." Harold gave the man a stern look.

Mr. Gordon smiled like a hyena. "Son, you have yourself a deal." He took the card and handed EJ the crystal, who slid it into his backpack.

Harold glared at Mr. Gordon. "Kids, it's definitely time to go."

Dylan hurried out of the house with EJ. "I can't believe you did that. Thanks."

EJ gave a sly smile. "No big deal. Besides, the card is only worth about thirteen dollars now. Hulk had gotten ahold of it and slobbered all over it."

Dylan laughed and gave his best friend a slap on the back.

Chapter Eight

The drive back from Sacatone was silent except for the occasional "Hmpf" and head shake from Harold, who was still disgusted that Mr. Gordon took EJ's baseball card even though EJ had told Mr. Gordon its real value.

Dylan couldn't keep the smile off his face as he thought about the fact they had the fire crystal. But then he wondered who put it in that cache to begin with? Was it Jessica? He'd have to ask Tera about that. Or was it someone else? Someone who knew that Mr. Paine had used geocaching as a way to keep it safe? He hadn't gotten a close look at the crystal yet. He'd have to check it for a tracking number when they got back to the house.

Suddenly a new thought sprang into his mind—were they going to tell Mr. Paine they had found another crystal? What if Harold told him about the rock first and Mr. Paine asked to see it? This time Dylan couldn't keep the crystal a secret from any of his friends. And technically, the crystal belonged to EJ since he traded for it. Telling Mr. Paine seemed like a good idea, and it might make up for the fact he and Kari still hadn't handed over the earth and wind crystals. But one thing about that plan bothered him—if he didn't have the fire crystal, how would they find out who its catalyst was? Even if he did keep it, he still had no idea how to find the person, but at least they could try testing it out. His smile faded when he thought about holding the fire crystal. He had hoped he might feel something, a shock or a zing up his arm like the girls talked about when they held their crystals. It had been warm, but it was that way for everyone. He hadn't felt anything...special.

Gloria was busy cooking dinner in the kitchen when they got back. She asked about their outing and invited them outside for an "afternoon snack," which was an entire spread of fresh fruit, cheese, and crackers. She poured them tall glasses of lemonade and went back to work while Harold laid down on the couch for his nap.

"Does your grandma always feed people this much food?" EJ popped four grapes into his mouth at once, filling his cheeks like a chipmunk.

"Pretty much. And there's always at least three homemade desserts at all times."

EJ's eyes bugged out and he tried smiling, leaving grape juice dribbling down his chin.

Dylan looked over his shoulder to make sure the patio door was closed so Gloria couldn't hear them talking. "Tera, are you going to tell your dad about the fire crystal?"

She picked apart the green leafy stem of a strawberry. "I think so. I promised I wouldn't keep any more secrets from him."

Dylan and Kari glanced at each other. Heat rushed to his face and he hoped his red mask of guilt wasn't forming. He didn't know how much longer he could keep the fact that he had the other two crystals a secret from Tera.

Kari quickly looked away from Dylan. "Maybe your dad will be able to figure out who the catalyst is if he has the crystal."

"Hey, don't I get a say? Don't forget, the rock is mine." EJ made a tower out of crackers and cheese slices.

Kari snatched a piece of cheese from the middle of EJ's tower, sending it tumbling. "What would you even do with the crystal?"

EJ re-stacked his cheese and cracker sandwich and then just stared at it.

Dylan noticed him rubbing his palm again. "Earth to EJ, are you okay?"

He seemed to snap out of it. "Yeah, I'm fine." EJ picked up part of his cracker tower and ate it like a sandwich.

"You didn't answer my question," Kari said.

"What was your question?" Cracker crumbs flew out of EJ's mouth as he talked.

"I asked what you would do with the fire crystal if you kept it?"

EJ frowned. "I dunno. Depends on what its power is."

Kari rolled her eyes. "We won't know what its power is until we find the catalyst. And we already know it's not me or Tera."

"Thank goodness," Tera mumbled.

"Then I'll just hang on to it until we find the catalyst," EJ said. "Or I could sell it."

"No way!" Dylan almost jumped out of his chair.

EJ laughed. "Take it easy. I'm just yanking your chain."

Dylan could hardly stand the thought of EJ being in charge of one of the crystals. "No offense, but you aren't exactly the best at keeping track of things."

"What do you mean?"

"You tend to...lose things." Dylan didn't want to hurt his friend's feelings.

"Like what?"

"Like your pet hamster," Dylan said.

"That wasn't my fault," EJ protested. "The little rodent chewed his way out of his cage. We never did find him."

"Exactly." If EJ couldn't find a living, breathing creature, there was no way he could hang on to a priceless crystal. Suddenly Dylan worried EJ had already lost the rock. "You do still have the crystal on you, right?"

"Pffft. Of course." EJ leaned over and reached into his backpack, rifling through bags of chips. "I swear I put it in here."

Dylan's heartbeat sped up. "Please don't tell me you lost it already!"

A wicked smile spread across EJ's face. "Nah, it's right here." He pulled out the rock and threw it into the air like a baseball.

"Don't drop it!" Dylan could picture it landing on the brick patio and shattering.

EJ set the crystal on the table in front of him. "See, I can hang on to things."

"OK, what about losing your homework every other day?" Kari pointed out.

"That doesn't count," EJ said. "Everybody loses their homework."

"I've never lost my homework." Kari sat back and crossed her arms.

"Well you're not normal," EJ said.

"I'm way more normal than you," Kari shot back.

"Oh really? You think it's normal to be a tornado whisperer?"

Dylan cringed. That seemed like a low blow, even for EJ.

Kari glared at EJ. "You're just jealous."

"Ha!" EJ sat back in his chair. "Jealous? Of what?"

"Of the fact that I can do something you can't."

"Whatever," EJ picked up another stack of crackers and cheese.

"You are and you know it," Kari said. "You wanted to be a catalyst, just like me and Tera, and you can't stand the fact that for once you're not special."

"Don't drag me into this," Tera said.

Kari wouldn't back down. "It's true. He thinks he's so great at baseball and can get away with stuff all the time, like not turning in his homework, while the rest of us have to work extra hard at sports and school just to keep up."

EJ's face turned red. "You don't think I work hard? Some of us aren't as smart as you, so we have to work ten times harder. And I have to work my butt off in baseball if I want to get a scholarship. No college is going to offer me an academic scholarship."

"They might if you didn't lose your homework all the time," Kari said.

EJ picked up the crystal and clenched it in his fist. "I'm glad I'm not a freak like you! I don't have to worry about anyone coming after me and trying to kidnap me."

"Knock it off, you guys," Tera said. "We're supposed to be on vacation."

EJ and Kari continued glaring at each other.

Suddenly EJ's expression looked pained, and he

dropped the crystal back on the table. "You know what? You can do whatever you want with the rock. I don't want it."

Relief flooded Dylan. He was a little surprised EJ gave up the crystal. But then EJ had never been that interested in the crystals to begin with. Dylan reached across the table and picked up the rock, happy to have it in his possession.

"Thanks, EJ. I'll give it to my dad after dinner tonight." Tera held out her hand in front of Dylan. He had to give it up after all.

"Good riddance." EJ pushed his chair back with a loud scrape against the patio and stormed inside.

"I swear, he's so sensitive," Kari said.

Dylan shook his head at her.

"What? He's the one who walked away, not me."

"You both owe each other an apology," Dylan said.

"I am not apologizing to that Neanderthal," Kari said. "He called me a freak!"

Dylan looked to Tera for help.

"I got this," she said. "You go see if EJ's okay."

Dylan got up and left the girls at the table. Tera could handle Kari. He would have his hands full with EJ. It'd take a miracle to get his hot head cooled off after all that.

He went into the house and found EJ in their bedroom lying face up on top of the covers, headphones on, eyes closed.

"Hey," Dylan said. EJ didn't respond. "Hey!" He nudged EJ's foot.

"Dude, leave me alone."

"Come on, don't be mad," Dylan pleaded.

"I'm not mad."

"I don't blame you. Kari went way overboard."

"I told you. I'm not mad."

"Then what's wrong?"

"Nothing. I just want some time alone." EJ still wouldn't look at Dylan.

"We're in a house with seven people. You don't get to be alone." Dylan waited a minute, but still no response except for EJ rubbing his palm again. "What's wrong with your hand?"

EJ finally glanced at Dylan. "Nothing. It's fine."

Dylan knew his friend was lying. "Let me see it." He grabbed for EJ's wrist.

"I said no!" EJ jerked his hand away.

"Come on, let me see it." Dylan tackled EJ on the bed and grabbed his wrists. EJ struggled underneath him. "Open your hands!"

EJ finally went limp. Dylan rolled off him and sat up on the edge of the bed. EJ sat up and put his hands in his lap. He slowly opened his fists. Both of his palms had angry red burns inside them.

EJ looked at Dylan, tears forming in his eyes. "This is what's wrong."

Chapter Nine

Dylan leaned toward EJ, comparing the two burn marks on his palms. They were identical. "When did that happen?"

"When we were sitting outside. I got mad at Kari for pestering me about being a catalyst, and all of a sudden the crystal got really hot. That's why I dropped it on the table and left."

Dylan remembered EJ's fight with Kari at Mr. Gordon's house. "Did it burn your other hand the first time?"

EJ nodded. "Pretty much." He tucked his hands underneath his legs. "Wait a minute, why do you have that mad scientist look in your eye?"

"Because I think I may be on to something." Dylan realized that both times the crystal had gotten hot, EJ had been arguing with Kari. "I hate to be the one to tell you this, but I think you are the catalyst."

EJ groaned and rolled his eyes. "Uh-uh, no way!"

"Think about it. Both times you got 'fired up' and both times you got burned."

"Fired up? Really? So my temper controls the crystal? If that's the case, then I'll end up setting myself on fire by the end of the day." EJ fell backward on top of the bed and covered his face with his arms.

Dylan sat on the bed, chewing his bottom lip. They

had to be missing something. It didn't make sense that the crystal's only power was to get hot enough to burn its catalyst. What good was that? EJ must be doing something wrong, which wasn't surprising. But how would they figure it out if every time EJ held the crystal, it hurt him? Dylan turned to face his friend.

"I think you should hold the crystal again, but stay calm while you do it. Just so we can see what happens."

EJ let his arms fall beside him on the bed. "This is exactly what I didn't want to happen. All of you guys using me as your guinea pig."

"Then we won't tell the girls about it." Dylan cringed as he said the words, hoping EJ would refuse. The last thing he wanted was to keep another secret from Tera.

EJ let out a big huff. "Fine. But just once. There's a small problem though."

"What's that?"

EJ sat up. "Tera has the crystal. She's going to give it to her dad, *remember*?"

Dylan winced. He couldn't ask Tera for the crystal without telling her why he needed it, and he had just promised EJ not to say anything. So that left one option— he'd have to sneak it away from her. He groaned at the thought. Why did everything involving the crystals have to include secrets and stealing? And why was he the one always keeping the secrets and doing the stealing? He looked at EJ's slumped body and knew why—because his friends were important to him, and he'd do anything to help them.

"I'll take care of getting the crystal from Tera as long as you promise to keep your temper under control and try your hardest to help me figure out how the crystal works."

EJ looked over at him. "This stuff means that much to you, huh?"

Dylan cracked a small smile. "Yeah, it really does."

EJ held out his hand. "Frankenstein, at your service."

Dylan laughed, and with a gentle grip, shook EJ's hand.

EJ lay back down on the bed and stuck his headphones back in his ears. Dylan got up to head back outside and see what the girls were up to. He went into the hall and rounded the corner toward the kitchen—then smacked right into Tera, who rounded the corner at the same time. Dylan's forehead collided with her chin, and she dropped the pile of stuff she had been carrying.

"Ow!" Tera staggered backward, rubbing her chin.

"Sorry! Are you okay?" Dylan felt like he had slammed into a brick wall but was more worried about having knocked out Tera's teeth.

"Yeah, I think so. Sorry, I didn't hear you coming." She bent down to gather everything that had fallen out of her beach bag—sunglasses, flip flops, and a book.

Dylan leaned over to grab a tube of sunscreen that had rolled against the wall and spotted the crystal nestled in the hallway's brown shag carpet. He looked over at Tera. She was busy stuffing everything back in her bag and hadn't noticed it. This would be the perfect time to take the crystal. He could slip it into his pocket and she'd never know. Dylan closed his fingers, raking the crystal into his hand.

"Oh no, where'd it go?" Tera muttered, digging through her beach bag. "I know I put it in here."

"What are you looking for?" Dylan cringed at how

fake his voice sounded.

"The crystal. I put it in my bag before coming inside. It must have fallen out just now. Help me look for it." She dropped her beach bag and crawled along the hallway.

Dylan got on his hands and knees and pretended to help her search even though the crystal was in his palm. His heart sped up and its beat felt like a drum in his chest echoing the word *liar, liar, liar*. He should just give it to her. Keeping another secret might actually kill him. He sat back on his heels, ready to confess.

"Tera?" Gloria's voice rang down the hall from the kitchen. "Can you be a dear and pick some oranges off the tree outside for me? I can't reach them and your grandfather is sleeping."

"I'm not sleeping! I'm just resting my eyes," Harold grumbled.

"Sure, Grandma!" Tera stood up and looked down at Dylan. "Maybe I dropped the crystal outside. I'll check when I go out to pick oranges." She added a smile. "Don't worry, I'll find it. I know you'd never forgive me if I lost it."

Tera walked down the hallway, and once she was out of sight Dylan fell forward until his forehead rested on the floor. He rubbed it back and forth on the shag carpet, wishing he could burrow down into it like a worm—like a slimy, dirt-eating, bottom of the food chain worm.

"Dude, what are you doing?" EJ whispered.

"Hiding." Dylan's voice was muffled in the carpet.

"You do realize hiding your head like a flamingo doesn't work."

"Ostrich."

"What?"

Dylan lifted his head and looked at EJ who was standing in the doorway of their bedroom. "You mean ostrich. Flamingos don't bury their heads to hide, ostriches do."

"Same thing. So did you get the rock or not?"

Dylan held out his arm and opened his hand that held the crystal.

"Well come on. Let's get this over with." EJ disappeared back into the bedroom. Dylan got up and followed him. Maybe if they could figure this out quickly, then he could give Tera the crystal and tell her he had found it in the hallway after all. Technically, that wouldn't be lying.

EJ stood in the middle of the room. He cracked his neck to each side and interlaced his fingers, stretching his arms out in front of him. "So how do we do this?"

Dylan scratched his head. "You need to be as calm as possible. Think of something…relaxing. Like puppies or bunnies."

EJ rolled his eyes. "You forgot to add unicorns and rainbows."

"I don't know! What makes you happy—besides food?"

"Dude, nothing makes me happier than eating."

"Fine. Close your eyes and imagine eating your favorite food." Dylan figured EJ would picture a huge banana split or an entire pepperoni pizza.

EJ closed his eyes and a smile slowly spread on his face. "Got it."

"Now hold out your hand." Dylan gently placed the crystal in EJ's open palm. "Keep picturing it—how it smells, how it tastes." The smile on EJ's face didn't budge. "Good. Don't move. You're doing great." Dylan sounded like someone trying to diffuse a bomb. He glanced at EJ's palm that held the crystal. It didn't look like it was getting redder from a burn. He could hardly see the burn mark at all, which gave him an idea. "Hold out your other hand."

EJ extended his other arm. Now he looked like a zombie. Dylan took the crystal from EJ's right palm and put it in his left palm.

"What are you doing?" EJ opened one eye.

"Just testing something. Go back to your food."

EJ shifted his stance and closed his eyes again. Dylan watched EJ's palm with the crystal, not saying a word. He blinked to clear his eyes—was the burn mark fading? He waited what he thought was a full minute then removed the crystal. EJ opened his eyes. Both boys bent their heads over EJ's open palms.

"Where'd they go?" EJ turned his hands over, examining both sides. "The burns are gone!"

Dylan grabbed EJ's hands and stared at both his palms—not a single trace of red. Not even a scar.

EJ pulled his hands away. "Woo hoo!" He twirled, running his hands through his hair and holding them in the air. "This is unbelievable! Fish, you're a genius!"

Dylan looked at the crystal in his hands. "Do you know what this means? Not only are you the catalyst, but you can use this to *heal* burns. I wonder if you can heal all burns, or just your own?"

"Who cares!" EJ danced around the room like an elf.

"But you have to stay calm for it to work. When you get mad, it burns you." And Dylan knew when it came to EJ, he was fired up about something most of the time.

Unless he was thinking about food, apparently. "So what were you imagining yourself eating?"

EJ stopped dancing and looked at Dylan with a goofy grin. "Only the best thing ever known to man. Taco Mac."

Dylan stuck out his tongue. "Do I even want to know what Taco Mac is?"

"Taco Mac is a macaroni and cheese casserole made with beef and salsa and topped with lettuce, tomato, sour cream, guac, black olives, and covered with tortilla chips. My mom makes it for me every year on my birthday."

"Remind me never to come over to your house for dinner on your birthday."

"Dude, you haven't lived until you've experienced the Taco Mac." EJ's face was so serious, Dylan burst out laughing, and EJ joined him. They were so loud they didn't hear the bedroom door open.

"What's so funny?" Tera walked into the room. She looked from EJ to Dylan and then down at Dylan's hand. Her expression fell. "What are you doing with the crystal?"

Chapter Ten

Dylan's throat tightened and heat rushed to his face. He knew red splotches were spreading across his face like footprints.

"He did it." EJ pointed at Dylan.

Leave it to EJ to rat out his best friend.

Tera looked at Dylan like he was a criminal.

"I…I…" Dylan could hardly form words. "I found it in the hallway. I was going to bring it to you. But EJ grabbed it from me. I had to wrestle him for it."

Tera crossed her arms and put all her weight on one leg. "Why don't I believe you?"

"It's true! EJ, tell her."

"You want me to tell her the *truth*?"

"Yes, tell her what happened." The last thing Dylan wanted was for Tera to think he was lying about finding the crystal. And it was true; he had found it in the hallway.

"Okay, if you say so, Fish." EJ cleared his throat. "It turns out I'm just as much of a freak as you and Kari."

Dylan gasped. "No! That's not what you're supposed to tell her!"

"Dude, you said to tell her the truth!"

"I didn't mean that! I meant to tell her the truth about how I found the crystal in the hallway!"

"Ohhhhhh." EJ plopped down on the bed. "Sorry."

Tera walked up to Dylan and poked him in the chest

with her finger. "Dylan Fisher, you better tell me what's going on right now, or I swear I will never, ever, speak to you again." Her emerald green eyes locked on to his and didn't move. Not even a quiver.

"Okay. I'll tell you everything." He took a deep breath. "We think EJ is the catalyst for the fire crystal."

Tera finally blinked. "How do you know?"

Dylan and EJ looked at each other. EJ raised his eyebrows as if to question whether or not it was ok to tell her. Dylan nodded.

EJ stood up from where he had been sitting on the end of the bed and held out his right hand. Dylan placed the fire crystal in EJ's palm, and as soon as it touched his skin, the crystal flashed bright red.

Tera let out a quiet gasp. "But...what does it—"

Dylan held up his hand. "Wait for it." He watched EJ's face, which showed no sign of pain. "Is it working?"

EJ shrugged. "It doesn't hurt yet."

"Why would it hurt?" Tera asked.

Neither boy answered. Dylan wondered if EJ was still too calm from their experiment a few minutes before. He needed to get EJ mad again.

"Boo!" Dylan lunged at EJ who jumped, stumbled over the corner of the bed, and fell onto the floor.

"Dude! What'd you do that for?" EJ scowled at him. "Ouch!" He dropped the crystal out his clenched fist and rubbed his palm. "Happy now? It worked."

"EJ, let me see your hand." Tera reached out and gently held his wrist, peering into his palm. "It burned you?"

EJ nodded and then pulled his hand away.

Tera turned toward Dylan. "What kind of power is

that? Why would a crystal hurt its own catalyst?"

"We don't know. We just found out about it." Dylan couldn't understand why Tera was acting like it was his fault EJ got burned. "But that's not all it does. C'mon, EJ. Show her the rest."

"There's more?" Tera took a step back like the crystal might burn her next.

EJ gave Dylan one more glare, and then he sucked in a deep breath and closed his eyes. He cupped the crystal in both hands.

"Just think of the Taco Mac," Dylan said.

EJ opened one eye. "I know, I got this." He stood with both eyes closed and swayed slightly. A glow radiated between his fingers.

"It's going to burn his hands to a crisp!" Tera said.

"No it won't. Just wait." Dylan hoped it would work again.

After a long 30 seconds, EJ opened his eyes. He looked like he had just woken up from a death nap. He looked at Tera, and then turned his gaze toward Dylan. EJ winked. "Boo-yah!" He dropped the crystal on the bed.

"Yes!" Dylan held his hand up, and EJ gave him a high-five, the burn mark on EJ's palm, gone.

"EJ, let me see your hand." Tera grabbed EJ's wrist and examined it, running her fingers over his palm. "I don't get it. One minute it burns you, and the next it heals you?" She looked at Dylan like she was pleading for an answer.

"I guess so." Dylan didn't know what else to say.

"But why?" This time Tera addressed EJ.

"How should I know?" EJ stretched over the side of

the bed and fished a candy bar out of his backpack that was sitting open on the floor.

"If the crystal can do that to you, can you make it do that to other people?" Tera asked.

EJ bit off half the candy bar, chewing it like a wad of gum.

Tera turned around and faced Dylan.

"We don't know," he said. "We haven't gotten that far."

"Well let's try it right now," she insisted. "We need to know exactly how it works."

"Time out," EJ said. "This monkey's done dancing for one day."

"EJ, this is important," Tera urged. "What if *you* get kidnapped by 4E Labs, and they hold a gun to your head and threaten to kill you if you don't tell them everything the crystal does?"

"Then it's sayonara, sister." EJ shoved the other half of the candy bar into his mouth.

Tera glared at him. "Fine. Then I'll just have to tell my dad that not only did we find the fire crystal, but that you're the catalyst." She stuck her hip out again and crossed her arms in front of her.

"Don't you dare!" A chunk of chocolate fell out of EJ's mouth. "Fish, don't let her."

"What makes you think I can stop her?" Dylan couldn't make Tera do or not do something. He couldn't make Kari, his sister, or any girl for that matter.

"I don't want your dad finding out and doing weird experiments on me like some sort of lab rat," EJ said. "Fish has already put me through enough."

"Hey, you agreed to it," Dylan said.

"My dad is not going to do experiments on you like a guinea pig," Tera said.

"Lab rat. That's way worse than a guinea pig," EJ said.

Tera shook her head. "Whatever. My point is he wouldn't do anything to you. He just needs to know about it. So he can protect you."

"Pffft. I don't need protecting." EJ waved her off. "In case you weren't paying attention, I've got super powers now."

"Ha!" Tera let out a snort. "Super powers that are not only out of your control, but they actually hurt you. Believe me, when 4E Labs comes after you, it won't matter what you do. You'll be helpless."

"I'll be fine. Besides, 4E Labs will never know about me because we're not going to tell anybody about it. Are we?" EJ stared at Tera like he was playing a Jedi mind trick on her.

She stared back at EJ for several seconds. "Fine. If I promise not to tell my dad that you're the catalyst, then can I give him the crystal?"

"How do I know you'll keep your promise?" EJ tried looking down at Tera, but she was a whole head taller than him.

"Because I don't lie," she said.

"Fish, do you vouch for her?"

Dylan rolled his eyes. "Of course I do. C'mon already. Just give her the crystal. She won't tell her dad about you."

EJ eyed them both. "OK, but if your old man so much as glances at my hands, you're both whale dung." He tossed the crystal at Tera. "I'm trusting you."

Tera smiled. "Thanks, EJ. I won't let you down."

EJ flopped back on the bed. "Now leave me alone. I need my beauty sleep before dinner."

Dylan followed Tera out into the hallway. He touched her elbow to stop her, and she turned around, inches from his face. "Thanks."

"For what?"

"For agreeing not to tell your dad."

She smiled and her eyes lit up the dim hallway. "I didn't do it for EJ."

Dylan gave her a confused look.

Tera laughed. "I did it for you, silly."

Heat rushed to Dylan's face. "You did?"

"Yes. I know you have some big plan in the back of your mind to figure out all this catalyst stuff."

Dylan's high disappeared. Tera thought he had some grand plan? Great. He had no idea what he was doing, and as soon as she figured that out, he'd be ancient history.

Tera hooked her arm in his. "Let's go tell the captain we found another crystal!" She guided him down the hall, and Dylan felt like a dog being yanked by a leash with all four feet splayed in front of him, resisting being taken to the vet.

He looked at Tera's hand that clutched the fire crystal. Maybe he could grab it and run back into EJ's room? But then what? He'd be right back where he started. Defeated, Dylan let Tera lead him into the living room.

Mr. Paine looked up from his paperwork. "I've been waiting for you two."

Chapter Eleven

Dylan's heart plunged to his knees. Why had Tera's dad been waiting for them? Did he already know about the crystal? About EJ? Maybe he had overheard them talking in the bedroom. Dylan looked at Tera for help.

"What's up, Dad?"

Mr. Paine leaned back in the small desk chair and crossed his arms. He looked like he was trying to figure out exactly what to say. Dylan shifted his weight from foot to foot while he waited.

Mr. Paine cleared his throat. "I need you both to tell me the truth."

Dylan's stomach barrel rolled.

"About what?" Tera's voice sounded higher than normal.

"About EJ," Mr. Paine said.

Dylan closed his eyes to try and calm his stomach.

"What about him?" Tera asked.

It was all Dylan could do to open his eyes while he waited for Mr. Paine to drop the hammer.

Tera's dad leaned forward and rested his forearms on the desk. "Did EJ really con a guy out of a valuable rock for a bubble gum baseball card?" Mr. Paine's eyes lit up like Dylan's sister's when she shared some silly gossip at the dinner table.

Dylan choked out a small chuckle in relief. "Yeah. It

was pretty awesome."

"Serves that guy right for trying to swindle some kids," Mr. Paine said. "I hope your end of the deal was at least decent."

Dylan glanced at Tera. She fidgeted with the crystal in her hand.

"Funny you should bring that up, Dad. We actually have something we wanted to tell you. It's about the rock EJ traded his baseball card for."

"Oh?" Mr. Paine's bushy eyebrows separated and rose like a drawbridge.

Tera placed the crystal on the desk in front of her dad. "Remind you of anything?"

Mr. Paine leaned over it, his nose inches from its surface. Then he picked it up and held it under the desk lamp, examining every facet. Finally he set it back down where Tera had placed it.

Dylan and Tera looked at each other, waiting for Mr. Paine to say something.

"Do you know what it is?" Tera asked.

Her dad looked at her. Dylan couldn't decipher what he was thinking behind his dark eyes.

"I know exactly what this is. What I don't know is why you're showing it to me?"

"Because you made us promise to let you know about anything that had to do with the crystals. I'd say this falls into that category." Tera's frustration was clear in her clipped tone.

"I appreciate that," Mr. Paine said. "But it doesn't do us much good unless we know about its catalyst too. I don't suppose you have any information on that, do you?" He turned his attention from Tera to Dylan.

"No, not at all, sir." Dylan shook his head, a little too vigorously.

"We're giving you the fire crystal, Dad, which is pretty amazing. I mean, what are the odds that we'd find it all the way out here in California, especially in some old guy's rock collection at his run down house, who we just happened to bump into? How are we supposed to know who the catalyst is too?"

It was all Dylan could do to keep a smile from forming on his lips.

Mr. Paine rubbed his forehead. "You're right. I'm sorry. Thank you for keeping your promise. Now I promise to keep this someplace...safe."

"Like with the earth crystal?" Tera asked.

Dylan's throat tightened. Tera and her dad still thought they had the real earth crystal, not the fake.

"Yes, I'll keep it with the earth crystal so we know where both of them are."

Tera smiled. "Sounds good to me." She turned toward Dylan. "Sound good to you?"

It didn't sound good to Dylan at all. But he wasn't about to let Tera or her dad know that.

"Sure," he said with more enthusiasm than he felt.

Mr. Paine nodded. He picked up his briefcase from the floor, set it on top of the desk, and clicked it open. He placed the crystal inside and quickly shut the lid, clicking it back in place. Without another word he put his briefcase back on the floor and went back to his paperwork.

Tera walked out of the living room and back down the hallway. "That wasn't so bad."

"I guess." Dylan shrugged.

"I'm going to get ready for dinner." Tera smiled and disappeared into her room.

EJ was napping in their room, so Dylan decided to go back outside onto the patio. He needed to be alone anyway. Even though Tera had kept her promise and had not told her dad that EJ was the catalyst, the fire crystal was now gone. Locked away forever. Dylan kicked a rock and watched it skitter across the concrete. He plopped into one of the patio chairs but stood up again, pacing along the circular perimeter of the paved stones.

Finally he wandered around to the front of the house. An old basketball pole was still cemented into the ground on one side of the driveway. Bits of ragged net hung from the rim, and the wooden backboard's faded paint had slivered. But it was still standing. Dylan thought he had seen a box of balls on one of the shelves in the garage. The oversized door didn't have a code, so he went back into the house through the front door.

Not wanting to disturb Mr. Paine again, Dylan walked quietly down the front hall to the door that led to the garage. It was already ajar, so he slipped through. Gloria's minivan sat in the middle of the garage, surrounded by shelves of boxes, tools, and buckets. Every inch of the place was stuffed. Dylan moved to get to the other side where he thought he saw the box of balls, and then stopped when he heard a deep voice.

"They either don't know, or they wouldn't tell me." Mr. Paine spoke in almost a whisper.

Dylan froze, and then squatted behind the minivan's front right tire. He saw Mr. Paine's shiny black shoes underneath on the other side of the car.

"Tera's definitely not the catalyst. She was holding

the crystal the whole time." Mr. Paine was on the phone, but with who? Jessica?

Dylan held his breath so he wouldn't make a sound.

"I have two of the crystals now. That gives us a lot of leverage." Mr. Paine paused. "I understand, Sir. If you want them, we can make the exchange when I get back into town."

Sir? So he wasn't talking to Jessica. It must be Colonel Thornton. And what did Tera's dad mean by "leverage?"

"I'm not going to risk taking them into the lab. Besides, there's no one there I trust to test them."

Dylan's heartbeat thrummed in his ears. Mr. Paine had said "lab." As in 4E Labs? Where Jessica worked under cover. But Mr. Paine just said he didn't trust anyone there. Dylan shifted his weight from one leg to the other to stop the cramp forming in his thigh.

"I say we just sit tight and take our time. The boy is good at sniffing out the crystals. I wouldn't be surprised if he finds the last two. And I'm confident he'll tell me when he does."

Anger balled up in Dylan's chest. Is that what Mr. Paine thought of him? Some sort of bloodhound he could use to hunt down the crystals and drop them at his feet? Not anymore. When Dylan did find the last crystal, he wouldn't hand it over to Mr. Paine, even if his life depended on it.

"I've got my eye on the old man. He's gone geocaching with the boy quite a bit, but his background check came out clean. I'll do another sweep of his house if needed."

Heat rushed to Dylan's face as he realized Mr. Paine

must be talking about Mr. Lyman. Dylan fought the urge to believe the thought nagging at his brain—that Mr. Paine and Colonel Thornton were secretly working for 4E Labs.

The thought flew around in Dylan's brain, making him dizzy. He lost balance for a second and grabbed the minivan's front door handle to steady himself. A blaring high-pitched alarm sounded, and the van's headlights flashed.

Dylan saw Mr. Paine's legs move on the other side of the car. Dylan scrambled to reach the back of the car. He peered around the bumper and saw Mr. Paine standing where he had just been crouched. Dylan pulled his head back and positioned his body behind the back tire in case Mr. Paine looked underneath the car. He hugged his knees to his chest and closed his eyes, hoping it helped make him smaller.

"What in the devil is all that raucous?" Gloria's voice shouted above the car alarm. A second later the blaring stopped.

"Sorry, Mom. I must have leaned against it. That old heap is sensitive."

"That better not be how you talk about me." Gloria gave a snorting laugh. "Come inside and get washed up for dinner."

"Be right there."

Dylan heard Mr. Paine's shoes softly click against the garage floor. A few steps, then silence. He didn't want to open his eyes in case Mr. Paine stood towering over him. Instead, he waited for Mr. Paine to say something.

Minutes passed. Dylan finally opened one eye. He didn't see anyone. Then he opened the other eye. No Mr.

Paine. Had he gone inside? Dylan could sense he was there. Was he playing a waiting game? If so, Mr. Paine would lose. Dylan used to hide from his sister for hours at a time.

Finally, Dylan heard more steps clicking against the garage floor followed by the hollow sound of shoes walking up the stairs into the house. The door closed with a thud.

Dylan let out a long breath. He hadn't been caught. But now he couldn't just walk into the house from the garage. Mr. Paine would know he had been in there. He'd have to go out the door to the back yard. But getting into the house unseen was the least of his worries. He had to figure out how to prove that Mr. Paine was working for 4E Labs. The only way to do that was to get the fire crystal back and make Mr. Paine admit it. And there was only one person who could help him get the fire crystal back: Tera.

Chapter Twelve

Dylan spent the next two days feeling like a character in a horror movie. Jumpy at every turn, especially around Tera and her dad. He kept tabs on where Mr. Paine was at all times, hoping he'd overhear another one of Mr. Paine's phone conversations, but nothing happened. He also kept going over in his head how he was going to tell Tera what he had heard. He never got past "Hey, Tera." What was he supposed to say to her? "Do you want to go grab a Big Gulp from the Mini Mart, and by the way your dad is secretly working for the enemy?"

Every time Tera looked back at him from the front seat and grinned during their road trip home, Dylan's stomach somersaulted. He could barely smile back at her knowing she'd be devastated by his news. But he had to tell her. And even though it would upset her, she'd want to do the right thing. She'd help him get the fire crystal back. He had at least eight hours before they were home and he had to worry about it. He couldn't tell her in the car in front of everyone.

Dylan felt someone kick the back of his seat. He opened his eyes and realized he must have fallen asleep.

"Fish, wake up. Pit stop." EJ climbed past him to get out of the car.

"Where are we?" Dylan looked out the window and saw nothing but flat grassy fields.

"Somewhere in Wyoming." Tera studied him. "Are you okay? You've been awfully quiet."

Dylan stared at her for several seconds, not sure what to say. Part of him wanted to blurt out everything he had heard her dad say. The other part of him could hardly form words. "I'm just...tired. From the trip."

Tera squinted her eyes like she didn't believe him. "Are you sure there's not something else bothering you?"

Dylan shook his head, not wanting to risk spilling his guts.

"You know you can tell me anything," Tera said.

"Uh huh."

"Like if you're secretly mad that I gave my dad the fire crystal."

"I'm not mad." Dylan tried to sound convincing.

"Promise?" Tera asked.

"Promise." Dylan felt the anxiety stirring in chest. He needed to get out of there. "Come on, let's catch up with the others." He ran inside the gas station convenient store and found EJ in the chip aisle.

"Dude, your face is as red as this can of Pringles." EJ shook the can. "What were you doing, running laps around the parking lot?"

Dylan wasn't about to explain things to EJ. "I'm just ready to get home."

"Me too. I can't wait to have the bed all to myself tonight. You're kind of a blanket hog."

A laughing snort escaped Dylan. "Me? You flop around worse than a flounder. If I didn't hang on to the blanket it'd be wrapped around you like a burrito."

Giggling came from the end of the aisle. Tera and Kari huddled together, whispering.

"I've had enough of them, too," EJ said.

Dylan sighed and grabbed a bag of chips even though he wasn't hungry. At least eating would give him something to do for a few minutes instead of obsessing over how to tell Tera about her dad.

Dylan spent the rest of the trip dozing off and on. It was dark by the time they turned down their street. Mr. Paine pulled into his driveway, and everyone slowly climbed out of the car and gathered their bags and pillows. EJ and Kari thanked Mr. Paine then walked across the street to their houses.

"Thanks for everything," Dylan said to both Tera and her dad.

"You're more than welcome, Dylan. Glad you were able to come along." Mr. Paine sounded sincere, but he didn't smile as he turned and walked into the house.

Tera did smile at him. "I'm glad you were able to come with us too."

Dylan managed a small grin back at her. "Well, thanks again." He hoisted his bag higher on his shoulder and turned.

"Hey?" Tera said.

Dylan stopped and glanced at her.

"Do you want to hang out tomorrow? Maybe see a movie or something?" She chewed on her bottom lip.

The idea of going to a movie with Tera was awesome. But there was no way Dylan could sit next to her for two hours and not bring up her dad. It would be torture. It was already torture. He'd have to tell her first. "Yeah, sure."

"Great! I'll text you in the morning." She waved and bounced a little as she turned to go into the house.

Dylan's bag felt like a sack of bricks as walked to his house next door. He didn't want to think about tomorrow. Right now all he wanted was to crawl into his own bed. Right after he had a big glass of milk and a slice of whatever dessert his mom was sure to have saved for him.

***

Sweat drips down Dylan's temple and rolls off his cheek. Heat blankets him, but he can't see where it's coming from. Dark grey clouds billow around him, filling his vision. They morph into disturbing shapes—a lion with a jester's head; a mouthful of razor sharp teeth clutching a sleeping baby. They ebb and flow like a lava lamp. But they aren't liquid. They aren't even clouds. It's smoke.

The scent of burning wood fills Dylan's nostrils, and a cough explodes from his lungs. Seconds later, quick flashes of orange, red, and yellow peek through the smoke, testing to see if it's okay to come closer.

Dylan covers his nose and mouth with his arm to stop the coughing. Crackling sounds grow louder with another sound, slightly softer but more high pitched. Screaming.

The smoke parts just enough for Dylan to see a familiar silhouette and a brief glimpse at the person's long, dark hair. "Tera!" he screams. But the growing roar of the fire swallows the sound. He tucks his chin into his chest and makes a run at the smoke. Smack! Dylan's head collides with a wall. Stunned, he shakes it off. He can still see Tera's outline several yards in front of him.

What did he run into? With one arm outstretched, Dylan walks forward. His hand comes against something solid. It's hot but doesn't burn. Glass?

He pounds his fits against it. "Tera!" The sound is muffled against the glass wall. Dylan can see and hear the flames from his side. Why can't she hear him? "Tera!"

The flames close around her on three sides like a teepee with an opening in the front. Dylan sees bright flashes of light in the center, right where Tera stands. She's holding something in her hands. The fire crystal.

Dylan runs back and forth feeling along the wall for a handle. His shirt is drenched in sweat and the coughing consumes him. He bends over to catch his breath. He can't give up. He has to try and save her. He looks back up, eyes burning. The fire is gone. The crystal is gone. Tera is gone.

Dylan woke up with his bed sheet stuck to his sweaty neck. He rolled over and reached for his phone on the night stand beside his bed. His eyes watered from the bright glare off the screen. It was already 9:00 am. Tera should be awake. He sent a short text.

MEET ME OUT FRONT IN 10.

Dylan got out of bed and threw on pants, a hoodie, and the Colorado Rockies baseball hat EJ had given him. He went downstairs and headed straight for the front door, not bothering to walk through the kitchen. Breakfast could wait. He had to talk to Tera and get it over with.

A chill in the morning shade of the front porch greeted him, but sun shone on the dead winter grass. He sat down on the front step to wait and felt the cool concrete through his athletic pants. He only waited a few minutes before Tera walked across the yard and sat down next to him.

"Hey, were you able to get some good sleep and recover from the trip?" she asked.

Dylan thought about his dream. "I slept, but I don't know how good it was."

"You missed EJ, didn't you?" Tera gave a sly smile.

"Yeah, right." Dylan laughed but cut it off short. He needed to be serious. "I actually have something I need to tell you."

"About EJ?"

"No, not about EJ. Well, kind of about EJ. I mean, it's more about you than EJ. Well, not you, exactly, more like about your dad."

"Dylan, what are you talking about? You're not making any sense."

Dylan took a deep breath and shook his head. He needed this to come out the right way. "When we were in California I overheard your dad on the phone, right after we gave him the fire crystal. At first I thought he was talking to Jessica, but then he called the person on the other end 'sir,' so I figured he was talking to Colonel Thornton." He stopped to get Tera's reaction. Her round, green eyes were full of interest.

"What were they talking about?"

"Your dad was telling Colonel Thornton about how we gave him the crystal but didn't say anything about a catalyst, and they agreed they should take it to the lab for testing but couldn't let anybody know about it." He stopped again.

"So?" Tera asked.

"So, they were talking about taking it to 4E Labs."

"I don't get it."

Dylan jumped up and stared in disbelief at Tera. "How can you not get it? Tera, your dad and Colonel Thornton are secretly working for 4E!"

Tera stared at him with a blank expression. Then she started laughing. "That's ridiculous! You can't assume all that just by listening to a one-sided phone conversation."

Dylan felt a twinge of embarrassment that she'd laughed at his conclusion. "It was obvious, Tera. Your dad even talked about Mr. Lyman and how he watches what he does."

Tera stood up and put her hands on her hips. "My dad works for the government. He watches everybody. Especially when it comes to the crystals and my safety."

Dylan didn't have time to argue with her. He knew what he had heard. "We need to get the fire crystal back. I need *you* to get the fire crystal back. We can't let your dad and the Colonel take it to 4E Labs and start testing it."

Tera took a step toward Dylan. She was still a whole head taller than him and looked down at him with narrowed eyes. "I'm only going to say this once to you, Dylan Fisher. My dad is *not* working for 4E Labs, and neither is Colonel Thornton. I will *not* get the fire crystal back, and I will *not* listen to one more word about any of this."

Even though she hadn't raised her voice, he winced at her outburst. He looked down, the weight of defeat slowly filling his body, toes first. He replayed the phone conversation in his head for the millionth time. He knew he was right.

"Your dad is going to meet the Colonel to give him

the crystal. If you won't get it back for me, will you at least try and find out when and where their meeting is going to be?" Dylan thought that was a perfectly reasonable request.

Tera's expression turned from quiet anger to… sadness. The corners of her eyes looked watery, and her chin trembled once.

"Goodbye, Dylan." She turned and walked down the steps.

"Tera, come on." Dylan watched her walked across the yard and into her driveway until she was out of sight. She didn't look back at him once.

Chapter Thirteen

Dylan stood on his front porch waiting for Tera to come back. How could she just walk off like that? Should he follow her and try to talk to her? His experience with Jordan told him that when a girl was mad, it was best to leave her alone. He could always send a text and apologize. His stomach grumbled. The text would have to wait. He needed to eat first.

He walked back into the house and the aroma of warm syrup hit him. His mom stood at the stove making pancakes.

"Morning, sweetie. I thought I'd make you a welcome home breakfast."

Dylan sat down at the table and took a long sip of orange juice. The tart carton juice was nothing compared to the fresh squeezed juice Tera's grandma had for them every morning in California. Mrs. Fisher set a plateful of pancakes, still steaming, in front of Dylan. Before he could take his first bite, the doorbell rang.

"I'll get it." He hurried to the front door hoping it was Tera. Disappointment filled his hungry stomach when he saw EJ's baseball hat.

"Dude, what's for breakfast?" EJ stepped into the entry and walked past him straight for the kitchen.

"Your ability to seek out food is scary." Dylan looked toward Tera's house one more time before closing the door and following EJ into the kitchen.

"Hi Mrs. Fisher, have room for one more?" EJ sat down in Dylan's chair and took a bite from his plate.

"Of course, EJ, just give me a minute and I'll have a fresh batch."

Dylan rolled his eyes and sat across from EJ who shoveled forkfuls of Dylan's pancakes into his mouth, not stopping to wipe the syrup that hung from his chin. "Don't they feed you at home?"

"Yeah, but that was an hour ago. I'm a growing boy."

"You're going to start growing *out* pretty soon," Dylan said.

Mrs. Fisher set a fresh plate down in front of him, and Dylan drowned it in syrup. He lifted his fork to take the first bite when something outside caught his eye. With his fork in mid-air, syrup dripping from the pancake bite, Dylan stopped and stared out the window that looked over his backyard into the creek below.

"What the...?" He set his fork down and stood up. A man dressed in khaki pants and a black jacket walked between his and Tera's house toward the creek. It was Mr. Paine.

"EJ, we need to go outside for a second."

"Dude, I'm not done eating."

"This can't wait. We have to go outside *now*." Dylan wanted to follow Mr. Paine. What if he was headed to the creek to give Colonel Thornton the crystals? This might be his only chance to catch him.

EJ didn't stop eating, so Dylan grabbed the fork out of his hand.

"Hey! Gimme that!"

Mrs. Fisher turned around from the stove. "Dylan,

let him finish eating. You can go outside when your guest is done."

Dylan ignored her and walked out back with EJ's fork still in his hand. EJ followed him like a dog.

"Dude, didn't you hear what your mom said? Your guest is still eating!" EJ grabbed for the fork.

"I'm sorry, but we need to go down to the creek. I just saw Mr. Paine walk down there, and I think he's going to do something with the fire crystal."

"So?" EJ made another attempt for the fork, but Dylan switched hands and held it away from him.

"So, I overheard Mr. Paine talking to Colonel Thornton when we were in California, and I think they're both secretly working for 4E Labs. I tried telling Tera, but she didn't believe me. So it's up to us to get the crystal back before they do something with it. And before they figure out you're the catalyst."

EJ's eyes grew as big as a Minion's. "What are we waiting for? Let's go follow him." EJ marched off the deck and across the back yard. Dylan sprinted to catch up to him. They reached the edge of the yard where it turned into the taller grasses that led to the creek bank.

Dylan stopped and looked around. The bare winter trees allowed him to see clear down the creek. He didn't see anybody. "Where did he go?"

EJ walked a few yards down the bank. "Are you sure he came this way?"

"Yeah I'm sure. But you were distracting me with your fork antics."

"Hey, I was hungry. Never come between a man and his fork."

Dylan scanned the entire creek, looking up and

down both sides. Where had Mr. Paine gone?

Suddenly he saw him between the trees, walking right toward them. "EJ, hide!" Dylan darted behind a tree and saw EJ dive behind a tree beside him. Dylan plastered his body against the tree trunk and closed his eyes, knowing it wouldn't do any good. He could hear Mr. Paine's footsteps crunching twigs and dead leaves as he walked up the creek bank. Then the crunching stopped. Was he standing right there? Dylan opened one eye, expecting to see Mr. Paine towering over him, arms crossed in front of his chest. Instead, he stared at the house at the top of the hill. Dylan looked to his right and saw EJ curled into a ball on the ground at the base of the tree he hid behind, his hoodie covering his head. Dylan peeked around his tree and saw Mr. Paine standing with his back to them—and he wasn't alone.

Even with her red hair pulled into a ponytail, Dylan recognized Jessica. She must have snuck into the creek from a different direction.

Mr. Paine hugged her and smiled. "It's so good to see you. The red hair suits you."

Dylan had known hair that bright had to be dyed.

"Richard, this had better be important. We can't risk being seen together." Jessica's voice was quiet, but it still carried through the creek well enough to be heard.

"It is. I have reason to believe that either Dylan or his friend EJ is the catalyst to the fire crystal."

EJ popped his head out from underneath his hoodie and peered around the tree. He turned and looked at Dylan with his jaw hanging open like a skeleton.

"Are you sure? How do you know?" Jessica's voice rose just like Kari and Tera's did when they were excited.

"There seemed to be an incident when the kids first got the crystal, and the boys act like they're hiding something. Dylan's not talking though."

EJ gave Dylan a thumbs up.

"We have to confirm it so we're sure. You need to get both of them to interact with the crystal." Jessica's voice was stern now.

Mr. Paine ran his hands through his thick, dark hair. "The problem is I don't what to look for. What does the fire crystal do when it's activated?"

"The earth crystal starts earthquakes, and the wind crystal causes wind storms, so I'm guessing the fire crystal starts fires."

Dylan glanced at EJ who was staring at his hands. Jessica was wrong—the fire crystal burned, but it also healed. They had never seen any flames come from the crystal.

Mr. Paine started pacing. "I can't risk hurting those kids. We have the crystal; let's just keep it locked up."

Jessica grabbed Mr. Paine's arm. "Can I see it first?"

Mr. Paine reached into his jacket pocket and held out the crystal. "The geologist confirmed it's authentic—the symbol in the middle doesn't appear to be man-made."

Jessica took the crystal out of his hand and held it toward the sky. "It's beautiful."

"The red in the center matches your hair." Mr. Paine grinned.

Dylan frowned. Why was Tera's dad being so nice to Jessica if he planned on getting rid of her? Was it all part of his horrible plot to get control of all four crystals for 4E labs?

"Don't change the subject, Richard. How are you

going to figure out which boy is the catalyst?"

"I'll have to figure out a way to get each of them to hold it and then see what happens. It shouldn't be too difficult. Dylan is like a moth to a flame when it comes to the crystals, and EJ is like one of Pavlov's dogs—offer food and he'll come running."

EJ popped up from his crouched position.

"Sit down," Dylan hissed. EJ's temper was going to blow their cover.

EJ's hands balled into fists at his sides and marched toward Jessica and Mr. Paine.

What was he doing? He had lost his mind! "EJ, no!" Dylan bent low and ran after him, hoping to stop him before it was too late. Mr. Paine and Jessica hadn't noticed them yet—they were still facing each other, talking. Dylan came to within a few steps of EJ then reached out and grabbed the hood on his jacket, yanking his friend backward. EJ whirled and batted Dylan's arm away, then turned back around and kept walking.

Oh no you don't, Dylan thought. With a few quick steps Dylan caught up to EJ again, and this time he wrapped his arms around EJ's waist. With all his strength he heaved EJ up and spun him toward the ground. They landed hard in a heap, Dylan lying on top of EJ—stunned he had actually managed to tackle him.

EJ struggled underneath Dylan's arms, but Dylan tightened his grip and pressed his body against EJ's chest to hold him down.

"Get off me!" EJ shoved Dylan by the shoulders and rolled out from underneath him. He scrambled up and straightened his jacket.

Dylan got up and brushed off his pants. "What are

you thinking? They're going to hear you!" He turned in the direction of Mr. Paine and Jessica, who were staring at the boys.

Jessica waved and started up the bank toward them. Mr. Paine shoved his hands back in his jacket pockets and followed, his facial expression stern and determined.

"Dylan, it's nice to see you again," Jessica said. "And you must be EJ." She held out her hand, and EJ shook it without responding.

"We were just talking about you boys." Mr. Paine didn't sound surprised to see them in the creek. "We need your help with something."

"I'm not the catalyst," EJ blurted. "You can't make me touch that thing."

Dylan groaned to himself. EJ had totally lost his cool.

"We tested it in California and nothing happened. You can even ask Tera and Kari. Come on, Fish, back me up here." EJ's clenched jaw and bug eyes didn't hide the fear in his voice.

"Yeah, totally. All four of us took turns holding the crystal and nothing happened. I swear." Dylan shouldn't have added the last part—he felt his face redden the second he said it.

"Then you won't mind showing us." Mr. Paine reached into his pocket and pulled out the crystal. He handed it to Dylan then took a step back and folded his arms in front of his chest, waiting.

Dylan gripped the crystal in his right hand. Its smooth sides warmed his palm. He looked at EJ who was gnawing on his fingernails. For a minute Dylan wished he was the catalyst so his best friend didn't have to stand there in agony. After several seconds he opened his palm. The crystal shimmered, but it didn't glow like the others had when activated. "See? Nothing."

Mr. Paine nodded. "Very well. Now it's EJ's turn."

Dylan turned and faced EJ, holding out the crystal. "Here. Prove to them you're not the catalyst and then we can go back to your house and get some of your mom's Taco Mac. Doesn't that sound good? I'm starving, aren't you?" He hoped EJ remembered their experiment in California.

It took several seconds, but a smile slowly spread across EJ's face. "Taco Mac. Yeah, that sounds awesome." He reached for the crystal but looked at Mr. Paine. "Give me the rock and I'll show you once and for all it's not me."

As Dylan placed the crystal in EJ's hand he sucked in a deep breath and took his time blowing it out. EJ picked up on the signal and did the same. His fingers wrapped around the rock like tentacles, and his eyes locked on Dylan's. His serious expression didn't change, but then the corners of his eyes twitched and his jaw clenched. The crystal must be getting hotter!

"Mmmm I can already taste your mom's Taco Mac—the cheesy noodles, chunks of beef, and crunchy tortilla chips on top." Dylan had to get EJ to focus back on food. He didn't dare look at Jessica and Mr. Paine.

EJ closed his eyes and a bead of sweat escaped down his temple. The hand holding the crystal started to shake. Then his entire arm shook. He was like a tea pot about to whistle.

"EJ, are you okay?" Jessica's voice was soft and calm.

95

"He's fine. Right, buddy?"

Tears streaked down EJ's cheeks. Dylan silently begged him to gain control.

"Now's not the time to be a hero, son." Mr. Paine's voice sounded full of genuine concern.

Jessica stepped toward EJ and cupped his elbow.

"Don't touch him! He's fine!" Dylan tried pulling her hand away, but she ignored him.

"Come on, EJ, let go of the crystal." Jessica turned his hand over and released his fingers. When she removed the crystal she gasped at the angry red burn branded into his palm.

"It's nothing, that mark was already there! He burned his hand on the stove in California!" Dylan yelled.

EJ's body slumped as he stared at his hand.

Jessica put her arm around him. "We need to get some ice on that."

"No we don't! He can make it go away! That's his power. Show them. EJ show them!" Dylan clamped his hand over his mouth as soon as he realized what he'd said.

"What do you mean he can make it go away?" Mr. Paine asked.

EJ finally spoke. "He means that when I'm not in control, the crystal burns my hand. But when I'm in control, it heals my hand. We did it in California." His voice was barely above a whisper.

"That's remarkable." Mr. Paine paced again. "The ability to both hurt and heal. We have to figure out how to harness that power and how all of these catalysts work together."

"Not now, Richard. We need to tend to EJ's hand."

"We don't need to. He can show us how to heal himself. Isn't that right, EJ?" Mr. Paine was like a mad scientist who had made a great discovery.

If EJ couldn't speak up, then Dylan had to. "No. He's not going to be your experiment. Leave him alone."

"Dylan, I'm not going to experiment on him, but I would like to see his healing capability. That's not an unrealistic request."

"It is if he doesn't want to do it. And I'm telling you, he doesn't want to!" Dylan's voice carried through the creek with a satisfying echo.

"Well right now, I don't think he has much of a choice," Mr. Paine said.

"Oh yes he does." Dylan heard EJ mumble something but ignored it. "And I say to leave him alone!"

"STOP IT!" EJ yelled and grabbed the crystal from Jessica. A flame in the shape of a cone shot up out of his hand. He screamed and ran toward the creek, sliding on his stomach at the bank and plunging his hand into the water. Crackling sounds rippled overhead. Dylan looked up and ducked as burnt pieces of bark rained down.

The trees above were on fire.

Chapter Fourteen

Within seconds, flames spread through the creek, catching tree after tree on fire like candles. Dylan cowered in place, his fear of natural disasters choking him more than the thick smoke that started filling his lungs. *Think, Dylan, think*! What were the procedures during a fire? Stop, drop, and roll was only good for putting out flames. But staying low and covering your mouth—that was good for escaping.

He dropped to a crawling position and covered his mouth and nose with the collar of his sweatshirt, which already reeked like a charcoal grill. A grey haze filled his line of vision, so he used his hands to follow the slope of the ground and started moving up the bank. Shouts stopped him, and he squinted, trying to figure out which direction they came from.

"Dylan! EJ! Boys where are you?" Jessica's high voice barely carried above the snapping of burning wood.

"I'm okay!" Dylan's throat burned as he inhaled a gulp of smoke and his voice turned hoarse. A dark figure moved in and out of the billowing clouds like a shadow, away from the creek—it had to be EJ. Dylan got off his hands and knees then crouched, following EJ farther up the bank. He caught up to him by the play set. They bent over, coughing, and both looked back at the creek.

A wall of orange and crimson flames with peaks like

the mountain range ran from one end to the other. The once white bark of the aspen trees were charred black. Thick smoke poured out of each cone of fire, reminding Dylan of the rush of steam from a dish hot out of the oven.

A figure moved in between the trees, her red hair as bright as the flames against the grey smoke.

"Jessica's still down there looking for us. We have to let her know we're okay." Dylan started back toward the creek.

"Mr. Paine will get her!" EJ yelled.

Dylan stopped. He had forgotten about Mr. Paine. He scanned the creek bank. Tera's dad wasn't anywhere. Was he looking for them on the other side? "EJ, get down here, now!"

EJ jogged back down the hill. "Hurry up before we all get burned to a crisp!"

The boys covered their mouths and noses again with their hoodies. The closer they got to the fire, the harder it was to see where they were going. The crackling was as loud as firecrackers on the 4th of July. Dylan lost his bearings. He had no idea where to look for Jessica.

Then suddenly she appeared through the smoke in front of them. "There you are! Oh thank God. We have to get out of here." The whites of her eyes were almost as red as her hair.

Dylan lowered his hoodie so she could hear him. "Where's Mr. Paine?"

Jessica's expression fell. "I thought he was with you!"

The boys shook their heads.

"You don't think..." She turned toward the raging

fire, shielding her eyes with her arm. "I have to find him!"

Before Dylan could say anything, she disappeared back into the billowing smoke.

He blinked rapidly, in part to take some of the sting out of his eyes, but also to make sure he had really just watched Jessica head toward the fire. Dylan felt a tug on his sleeve.

"Dude, we have to get out of here!" EJ's eyes were the only part of his face not covered by fabric, and the whites were rimmed with red.

Dylan couldn't make his legs move—how could he just leave Jessica and Mr. Paine? What would Tera say when she found out he had let them be swallowed up by a fire? She'd never forgive him. He'd never forgive himself.

"I have to go after them." Dylan felt his lips move, but he couldn't hear the words above the fire.

"What?" EJ's voice sounded far away even though he was inches from Dylan's face.

"I said, I have to go after them!" Dylan shouted into EJ's ear.

"You've lost your mind! There's no way I'm letting you go in there!" EJ coughed out the last words.

"They might need our help. I'll come back if it gets too bad, I promise." Dylan pulled his collar back up over his mouth and nose, squinted his eyes to keep as much smoke out of his eyes as possible, and ducked his head as he started off in the same direction as Jessica.

A few feet into the smoke and he was blinded and coughing. Which way would Jessica have gone? The creek had to be straight ahead. Maybe it wasn't as bad there because the trees were mostly along the bank. And maybe the fire wasn't as bad on the other side of the creek. He had to keep going and find out.

Dylan took several more steps and then his right foot wrenched and twisted, filling his shoe with water. When he crouched, he could barely see the dark ripples of the creek water. He fell onto his knees and crawled through the icy current, the sharp cold a welcome relief from the intense heat. Smoke surrounded him, so Dylan kept his eyes closed and let the water guide him. For a few seconds the heat let up, and he thought he was almost to the other side of the creek. His hands felt hard ground so he scrambled up the bank and stood, squinting through more thick smoke.

"Jessica! Mr. Paine! Are you over here?" His voice came out hoarse. "Jessica!" He sputtered—a sharp pain jabbed his throat—and he doubled over.

He felt a hand grasp him by the arm. "Did you find them?"

Dylan looked up into EJ's soot-smeared, sweaty face. Had he followed Dylan to the other side of the creek? Why weren't EJ's pants wet from going through the water? "I thought for sure they'd be over here."

EJ shook his head. "I've been waiting here the whole time and didn't see anybody."

Dylan's chest tightened. Had he just crawled in a *circle*? "You mean I'm back where I started? Then they're still out there!"

"I'm not letting you go back again!" EJ squeezed Dylan's arm even harder and jerked him toward the hill.

The muscles in Dylan's legs finally gave out, and he let EJ take over.

They had walked a few feet when a loud crack

sounded overhead. Both boys stopped and looked up just in time to see a large limb engulfed in flames swing down off a tree. EJ spun Dylan by the arm he was holding and flung him forward as the limb crashed onto the ground between them.

Within seconds the flaming limb had ignited the dry grass and leaves around it, and a wall of fire separated the boys. Angry flames distorted EJ's face and sucked the sound out of Dylan's screams.

He lunged toward the fire, but the searing heat held him back. His brain kicked in, preventing him from making the fatal move of jumping into the wall of flames.

"EJ! Get out of there!" Dylan could barely see EJ's dark form on the other side of the flames, and then in the next instant he was gone. "EJ! No!" He ran up and down the fire's path, looking for a way around it so he could reach EJ, but he was blocked on all three sides by flaming trees. The heat and smoke pushed him back, forcing him farther up the bank.

Dylan fell backwards into a sitting position on the hill. He stared at the fire, unable to accept what he saw — what had just happened. His best friend, trapped in the flames…just like Tera in his dream. Only this was real — this nightmare was actually happening.

He heard a faint voice coming from behind him, calling his name. It was a girl's.

"Dylan! Are you okay?" Tera threw her arms around his neck from behind, burying her face in his shoulder. She squeezed him tight before turning to face him. "The firefighters just arrived. The whole neighborhood is up there. The Millers called it in and said they saw you and EJ down here. Where is EJ?" She looked around them.

"Dylan? Can you talk?"

He couldn't focus on her. He couldn't focus on anything. His throat felt like someone had shoved a handful of pine needles down it. His lips parted but couldn't form words. He pointed one index finger at the fire.

Tera's gaze followed his finger. "Oh Dylan, no." She put a hand over her mouth. Her eyes filled with tears.

The bowling ball in Dylan's stomach almost ripped out when he thought of Mr. Paine and Jessica. What would Tera do when she found out they were trapped in the fire too? Dylan closed his eyes, hoping someone— or something—would make everything go away... including him.

"Over here! There's someone trapped in the fire!" Tera yelled.

Three firefighters in long coats and smoke masks ran toward them, pulling a fire hose. One of them knelt beside Dylan and removed his mask.

"Can you stand up?"

Dylan didn't move. Even if he could he didn't want to. He wasn't going anywhere until they found EJ.

The firefighter pulled out a walkie talkie and called for a medic. The other two held the fire hose steady as a gush of water rained down over the creek.

Tera ran up to them. "What are you doing? Someone's trapped in there! You have to go in and find him!"

"We can't get any closer than this until we get the fire under control. The best thing you can do right now is to go with your friend and get to safety. I'm sure your folks are worried about you."

Tera returned to Dylan and the first firefighter, who

had placed his mask over Dylan's face. "They need to put out some of the flames before they can go in after EJ. But they'll find him. They have to." She grabbed Dylan's hands and squeezed.

He hoped she couldn't see the tears running down his cheeks from behind the mask.

Two medics ran down the hill carrying a stretcher. They picked Dylan up under his arms and hoisted him onto it. "Your parents are going to be happy to see you," one of them said.

"Did you happen to see a really tall man with dark hair up there?" Tera asked. "My dad wasn't home when all this happened, and I couldn't get a hold of him on his cell. I don't want him to be worried."

"There's a group gathered up there, but I don't recall seeing anyone with that description." The medics lifted the stretcher and started up the hill.

"I wonder where he could be?" Tera mumbled, walking beside them.

Even through the mask and haze Dylan saw the worry in Tera's eyes. She had to know the truth. He reached up and adjusted the mask so it rested on top of his head.

The medics stopped. "Is something wrong?"

Dylan motioned for Tera to come closer. His throat felt like he had eaten an entire jar of jalapeño peppers — there was no way he could talk above a whisper. Tera leaned down so her ear was inches from his mouth. He closed his eyes so he didn't have to see her reaction.

"Your dad..." he winced at the burning pain in his throat. "Jessica..."

"What about my dad and Jessica?" Tera's voice

wavered.

"They're with…" Dylan felt the panic, hurt, and tears bubble up from his stomach into his chest like a volcano about to erupt.

"Who are my dad and Jessica with, Dylan?" She sounded angry, and Dylan kept his eyes squeezed shut.

He gripped the edges of the stretcher, bracing himself for the searing pain that uttering the next two letters were going to cause. "EJ."

Chapter Fifteen

Dylan expected Tera to scream or cry in response to the news that her dad was trapped somewhere in the burning creek. When he didn't hear her say anything after several seconds, he opened his eyes. The only faces he saw were the two medics carrying his stretcher.

He sat up. "Where she'd go?" he managed to ask. Then he spotted her with the firefighters, pointing toward the flames and waving her arms around. Dylan lay back down. His throat was too prickly to attempt to yell for her, and he knew he didn't have the energy to get off the stretcher and go after her. Instead he closed his eyes and let the rocking motion of the medics carrying him up the hill soothe his nerves.

As soon as they reached the street a swarm of bodies circled him.

"Dylan, honey, can you hear me? Are you okay?" His mom grabbed his hand and squeezed. He nodded but still didn't open his eyes. "I'll ride in the ambulance with you to the hospital. Dad will meet us there. Where did Tera go?"

"The young girl is still down there with the firefighters. It seems there may be several people trapped in the creek," said one of the medics.

"Oh dear. Who was down there?"

This time Dylan opened his eyes and couldn't keep

the tears from rolling down his cheeks. "Mr. Paine and EJ." He didn't want to explain to his mom who Jessica was.

"Oh dear," his mom said again.

The medics lifted the stretcher into the ambulance and helped Mrs. Fisher inside. Before they closed the doors, the sound of sirens blared beside them, and another ambulance pulled up.

"We got a call you needed some extra help here," a male voice said.

"There could be more victims still in the creek," the medic said.

At the word 'victims' Dylan's stomach seized. His mom gripped his hand tighter. He lifted his head to look out the back of the ambulance and saw Jordan and his dad. His sister smiled and waved.

"We're right behind you, buddy." Mr. Fisher gave him a thumbs up.

The ambulance doors slammed closed and Dylan laid his head back down.

"Just rest," his mom said.

The medic placed a mask over his nose and mouth and told him to breathe normally. Cool air filled his lungs like he had been under water and finally came up for a breath. He heard his mom and the medic talking but tuned them out. All he wanted to do was fall asleep.

What felt like seconds later the ambulance doors opened and the medics rolled Dylan through a set of sliding doors. He knew he was at the hospital when he opened his eyes and saw white walls and bright fluorescent lights overhead. They took him into a small room and transferred him to an exam table. He still wore the oxygen mask and didn't want to take it off.

A nurse took his blood pressure while a doctor shined a light into his eyes and listened to his heart.

"It appears to be smoke inhalation, but I've seen worse. Keep the oxygen flowing and we'll get him something to help open up his airways. You are a very lucky young man."

Dylan took a deep breath of the oxygen coming through the mask. His eyes felt full of scratchy sand so he closed them. But seconds later they popped open when he heard shouting in the hall outside his room.

"Alert the burn unit! We're gonna need a lot of help here!"

Dylan propped up on his elbows and saw several doctors and nurses crowded around a gurney, their faces pale and serious as their hands and arms hurried to help whoever was in trouble.

"Has anyone contacted the boy's parents?" one of the doctors asked.

"They're on their way," said a nurse.

"Good. There might not be much time."

"Oh no," Mrs. Fisher whispered. Dylan had almost forgotten she was sitting in the room next to him.

One of the nurses left the group and Dylan caught a glimpse of the person on the gurney. He saw his hand, but the fingers were covered in angry red splotches with black char marks where skin should be. Then Dylan saw the person's arm, which was covered by pieces of blue fabric—the rest had been burned away. A feeling of horror settled over him when he realized what the fabric had once been. EJ's blue hoodie.

Dylan leapt off the table and tore the mask off over

his head.

His mom tried to grab him. "Where are you going? Lay back down!"

He shrugged her off and charged into the hall, prying his way between doctors and nurses. They didn't even seem to notice him.

Dylan stared down at the person on the gurney. The face was wrapped in white gauze, but the thin nose and plump bottom lip were definitely familiar, and he let out a cry for his friend.

"EJ!"

At the outburst, one of the doctors turned toward Dylan. "You can't be out here. Someone help this boy back to his room."

A nurse put her arm around Dylan and tried to lead him away from the gurney.

He grabbed a corner of the sheet covering EJ. "No! That's my best friend! I have to help him!" Dylan sobbed.

"The best way you can help him is by giving the doctors room to work," the nurse said. "Come on, there's nothing you can do." She gripped his shoulders tighter.

Dylan let the sheet slip from his hand and let the nurse guide him. But he looked over his shoulder at EJ the whole way back to his room. His mom stood by the table, clutching Dylan's hoodie.

"I heard," she said softly. "I'm so sorry. EJ will receive the best care possible though." She covered Dylan's shoulders with his hoodie. "You're shivering."

He pulled it closer around him, unable to get the image of EJ's burnt hand out of his mind. What would happen to him? Would he be scarred forever, or worse — die? It was all the stupid crystal's fault. Why did EJ have to lose it and start that creek on fire? Why couldn't he control his power? If he had, none of this would have happened. He wouldn't have gone into the fire and been burned. He'd still be okay.

Suddenly, a thought jolted Dylan. He tore off his hoodie and pulled out the pockets. It was still in there—the fire crystal. He ran back out of the room into the hall. It was empty. A nurse sat behind the desk.

"Where'd they take him? The burn victim?" he asked.

The nurse gave him a sympathetic look. "They took your friend to the burn unit."

"Where is that?" Dylan looked up and down the hall.

"It's on the fourth floor…"

Dylan sprinted toward the elevator.

"But you can't go up there!" the nurse called after him.

He punched the elevator button over and over. "Hurry up." Finally it dinged and the doors opened. He was relieved to see it empty and stepped inside, holding the number four button down. Just as the doors closed, both his parents appeared, their mouths gaping. "I'll be right back!" he called as the elevator shut.

He got off on the fourth floor and followed the signs to the burn unit. A nurse walked by, pushing an old lady in a wheelchair. She gave him a questioning look, and Dylan paused in front of the restroom door until they turned into a patient room. He kept walking down the long hall, which went on forever, and finally he faced the large double doors with a sign above that said "Burn Unit."

The area was small—a nurse's station in the middle

surrounded by rooms. It reminded Dylan of the classroom pods at school. Nobody was at the nurse's desk. He peeked into each room as he walked by. Most of them were dark and deserted. Except for one.

He recognized the nurse who had escorted him back to his room. She dabbed clear goop on EJ's body, which looked like a mummy wrapped in toilet paper. A doctor stood at the foot of his bed, typing on a laptop.

"Keep applying that until his parents get here." The doctor shook his head. "There isn't enough healthy skin to do grafts. I'm surprised he's held on this long." He flipped the chart shut and turned to walk out of the room.

Dylan pressed his back against the wall. The doctor went down the hall in the opposite direction and didn't notice him.

How am I going to get in there? Dylan thought. He looked at the crystal in his hand. It was EJ's only hope.

The doors to the unit opened with an electronic whooshing sound, and EJ's parents hurried through. They ran past the nurse's desk, glancing in each room. Dylan stepped away from the wall so they'd see him.

Mrs. Doyle went straight for him, wrapping Dylan in a hug. She pulled away, her face splotchy and her wet eyes rimmed with red. "Where is he?"

Dylan pointed to the room. He followed Mr. and Mrs. Doyle inside but only a few feet. He knew they needed to see him.

"I'll give you a few minutes," the nurse said. She stared at the floor on her way out and didn't pay attention to Dylan.

EJ's mom stood on one side of the bed and his dad on the other. They each looked for a place to touch him, but every inch was either wrapped in gauze or burned. Neither of them spoke, and Mrs. Doyle quietly started crying.

After a few minutes EJ's dad wiped his nose with his sleeve and turned toward Dylan. "How did the fire start?" His voice was gentle.

Dylan knew Mr. Doyle wouldn't believe the truth, and he didn't want to blame EJ. "I have no idea."

Mr. Doyle nodded. "I'm glad you're okay. Have you had a chance to see him?"

Dylan shook his head, and Mr. Doyle stepped aside. Dylan approached EJ, unsure what to do.

"I bet he'd like it if you'd talk to him," Mrs. Doyle said with a sad smile.

What was he supposed to say? Could EJ even hear him? He had to say something.

"You're gonna be okay, buddy. I promise."

Mrs. Doyle put her hand over her mouth and stifled a sob. She ran out of the room.

"Sorry, did I say something wrong?" Dylan hadn't meant to make things worse.

Mr. Doyle put a hand on Dylan's shoulder. "Not at all." Then he walked to the window, put his hands on the ledge and dropped his head.

With Mr. Doyle's back turned to him, Dylan knew he had a chance to give EJ the crystal. He slid it next to EJ's burned hand and carefully lifted his fingers so they wrapped around it. He pulled the sheet up over it, hoping the nurse wouldn't see it right away.

Dylan leaned over so his lips were inches from EJ's ear. He glanced at Mr. Doyle to make sure he wasn't watching. Then he thought of the one thing he knew EJ would understand if he could hear him. "Taco Mac."

Chapter Sixteen

The next morning Dylan woke up in a coughing fit. His lungs burned like he was still inhaling smoke from the fire. He pounded his chest and staggered to the bathroom, desperate for a drink of water. When he finally put his lips to the glass and sipped, the cold liquid soothed his throat with such relief, he drank cupful after cupful until he felt bloated.

Dylan dragged himself back to his bed and flopped down on it, covering his face with the pillow. Had yesterday really happened? It had. And EJ was still in the hospital, fighting for his life. EJ! Dylan sat up, remembering he had given EJ the fire crystal. He needed to see if it had worked!

He grabbed clothes off the floor, threw them on, and raced downstairs. His parents were still in their robes, drinking coffee.

"How are you feeling, sweetie?" Mrs. Fisher asked. "I heard you coughing again."

"I'm fine. Can we go to the hospital? I need to see EJ."

Mrs. Fisher stood up and wrapped her arms around Dylan. "We know you're worried about him, but the best thing we can all do right now is let him rest, be with his family, and let the doctors do their job."

Dylan wriggled free of his mom's embrace. "You

don't understand. I have to see him."

His parents exchanged looks like they were having a private conversation. His dad nodded.

Mrs. Fisher sighed. "If it's that important to you, I can take you after breakfast. Why don't you see if Tera and Kari want to go too? I'm happy to drive everyone."

Dylan didn't stick around to thank her. He ran back to his room to text the girls.

HEADING TO THE HOSPITAL IN 30 MIN IF YOU WANT A RIDE.

Kari was the first to text back. BE THERE IN 20.

He waited for Tera to text next. Five minutes went by but no response. Anger swelled in his chest like a balloon. He knew she had every right to be mad at him, for several reasons, but couldn't she put that aside at a time like this?

Five more minutes and still nothing. He decided to try again.

ANY OTHER TAKERS??

Another five minutes and still no response. Fine. If she wanted to be that way, so be it.

Dylan went back downstairs to wrangle his mom. She was not a morning person and knew she needed two cups of coffee before doing anything.

"I guess it'll just be me and Kari," he said. "She'll be here in 10 minutes."

"Then I had better throw something on. Tera isn't coming?"

Dylan shrugged. "I guess not." Mrs. Fisher took her last sip of coffee and Dylan reached for her mug. "I'll put this in the dishwasher while you get dressed."

Mrs. Fisher smiled. "You really care about EJ, don't

you?"

"He's my best friend, Mom. Even when he drives me crazy."

Mrs. Fisher disappeared upstairs. Dylan stuck the mug in the dishwasher without rinsing it, and the doorbell rang. He ran to the door to let Kari in.

"Hey." Kari's curly hair blew across her face in the breeze. "How are you feeling?"

"Ok. Did you hear back from Tera?"

"Nope. I tried calling too, but she didn't answer. Is everything good there?"

Dylan didn't know how to answer that so he just shrugged.

Mrs. Fisher came downstairs. "Hi Kari, nice to see you, dear. Are you both ready to go?"

"Yep, thanks for the ride, Mrs. Fisher." Kari smiled, and Dylan was glad she was going with him. He didn't like hospitals, and he really didn't like seeing his best friend in one.

The ride there was silent except for the light jazz songs playing on Mrs. Fisher's favorite radio station. Normally Dylan changed the channel, but this time he didn't care. All his thoughts were consumed with wondering whether or not EJ had started to heal from the fire crystal. With burns that bad, it would probably take days for it work, but Dylan was willing to wait as long as it took.

They parked in the hospital's visitor lot and made their way inside to the main elevators. Dylan pushed the button for the fourth floor. The ride up felt like 40 floors. When they got off the elevator he led Kari and his mom straight to EJ's room. Mr. and Mrs. Doyle were there, still wearing the same clothes as yesterday. A nurse stood at EJ's bedside, changing the bag of fluid attached to his I.V. Two additional people sat in chairs against the far wall: Mr. Paine and Tera.

Mrs. Fisher greeted everyone and walked up to Mrs. Doyle to give her a hug. "How is he doing?"

Mrs. Doyle wiped a tear from her cheek. "No change."

Dylan tried looking at EJ but couldn't see around the nurse. "Are you sure?"

"I'm afraid so, honey," Mrs. Doyle said.

Dylan wondered if the night nurse had found the crystal in EJ's hand and taken it away. He needed to find out. What was taking her so long with that I.V. bag?

Kari walked over to stand next to Tera. "I tried calling you to see if you wanted to come to the hospital with us."

"Sorry, I left my phone at home, and my dad wanted to come early to see how EJ was doing."

Even though Tera didn't look at Dylan, her answer made him feel a little better about her not responding to his text.

The nurse finally left the room. Dylan approached that side of the bed. EJ's hand was underneath the blanket. He'd either have to reach in and feel for the crystal, or he'd have to pull back the covers. Both seemed awkward.

"Feel free to talk to him," Mrs. Doyle said.

Dylan swallowed hard. Everybody stared at him. He had no idea what to say. "Hey...dude." Heat rushed to his face. He swallowed again.

Tera walked over to the other side of the bed. She put her hand gently on EJ's bandaged arm. "Hey, EJ, it's

Tera. And Dylan and Kari too. We're all here. Waiting for you to wake up and make us laugh."

The adults smiled and started talking quietly together again. Dylan placed his left hand on EJ's arm like Tera. He slowly slid his right hand underneath the blanket until he felt EJ's fingers. Then he felt underneath EJ's hand and brushed against something solid. It was warm and smooth. It had to be the crystal. Dylan slowly drew the blanket back, glancing at the adults. They weren't paying attention to him. Tera and Kari gave him questioning looks, but he kept going. Finally EJ's hand came into view. Dark red burns still covered the top of it.

"That can't be right," Dylan whispered. He tried pushing back the edge of the gauze that wrapped around EJ's arm to see if it was still burned too.

"What are you doing?" Tera whispered.

Dylan didn't answer. He readjusted the crystal so that EJ's hand completely covered it, and then pulled the blanket back up over his arm. He looked at EJ's closed eyes. "Come on, buddy."

The nurse walked back in and stood at the foot of the hospital bed. "The doctor is about to make his rounds. Could everyone step outside except for EJ's parents?"

"Of course," Mrs. Fisher said. "Why don't I go down to the cafeteria and bring you both back some fresh coffee?"

Mr. and Mrs. Doyle thanked Mrs. Fisher, who ushered everyone else out of the room.

"Care to join me?" she said to Mr. Paine. Then she turned to Dylan. "When we get back, it's probably best if we leave and let EJ rest." She and Tera's dad walked down the hall toward the cafeteria. Dylan, Kari, and Tera sat down in a waiting area by the nurse's station.

Dylan leaned back and covered his face with his arms. "I can't believe it's not working," he mumbled.

"What were you doing in there?" Tera asked.

He let out a long sigh. Maybe he should just tell them? If EJ didn't get better none of this would matter anyway. He had nothing to lose.

"I was checking to see if EJ's burns had healed."

Kari wrinkled her nose. "He's burned over most of his body. There's no way he'd heal that fast."

"Under normal circumstances, no, but EJ isn't... normal," Dylan said.

Kari chuckled. "Well we know that."

"What Dylan means is, EJ is like...us." Tera motioned toward herself and Kari.

"So he's a...girl?"

Dylan let out a laugh. "No, he's not a girl. He's a catalyst. For the fire crystal."

Kari's mouth dropped open. "No way! EJ's a catalyst? How do you know? What's his power? Wait, why didn't anyone tell me?"

"Shhhh!" Dylan looked around to make sure nobody was listening.

"I found out by accident," Tera said. "When we were still in California."

"You've known for that long?" Kari raised her voice again.

"Shh! Seriously, Kari, keep it down," Dylan hissed.

"They made me promise not to say anything," Tera said. "I hate keeping secrets, but this time I had to. I'm sorry."

Kari and Dylan exchanged looks. He knew she was

thinking about the fact they were both keeping a secret from Tera—that Kari had the wind crystal.

"It's ok. I totally get it." Kari's cheeks flushed. "So what does the fire crystal do?"

Tera looked toward Dylan.

"When EJ gets mad, it burns him," he said. "But when he concentrates, he can get it to heal the burns too."

"Did he start the fire in the creek?" Kari asked.

Dylan nodded. "But he didn't mean to. It was an accident, and it got out of control. I was able to get the crystal back from Mr. Paine, and I thought if I gave it to EJ in the hospital, it would heal his burns, just like it did when we were in California. But this time it didn't work. I don't know if his burns were too bad, or what." He shrugged and stared at the floor.

"Maybe it just hasn't been enough time?" Kari said. "Or maybe EJ needs to be awake in order for it to work? There has to be some way around it. We just need to figure out a way to help the crystal do its job."

They sat in silence for several minutes. Dylan racked his brain trying to come up with something. "What about bringing in a psychic? They're supposed to be able to talk to the dead. Maybe they can talk to the unconscious and tell EJ what he needs to do?"

"Psychics are con artists," Kari said.

Dylan scowled. "Well at least I'm trying to come up with something. You two are the ones with powers; can't you put your heads together and figure out a plan?" He felt useless at this point.

Kari's face lit up. "You might be on to something."

"You just said psychics are hacks," Dylan snapped.

"No, not that. What you said about us working

together. What if the crystals and catalysts could somehow work together?"

"That's not a bad idea, but there's just one problem," Tera said. "We don't have the other crystals."

Dylan and Kari exchanged looks again. "Actually, we do," Kari said slowly. "I'm afraid I've been keeping a secret from you too. I have the wind crystal." She pulled the necklace out from underneath her sweater.

Tera gasped. "Where did you find it?"

"It showed up on my birthday, and I thought it'd be safer if I just hung on to it. Are you mad?"

"No I'm not mad! That's amazing!" Tera lifted the crystal pendant and examined it.

"Well then I hope you won't be mad when I tell you another secret," Dylan said.

Tera turned around and faced him. "What is it?"

"I still have the real earth crystal. The one your dad has is the fake." He gave a hopeful grin and waited.

Tera stood silent for several seconds. Dylan couldn't read her expression. Was she about to freak out? Storm off? Never talk to him again? His stomach balled up and a dizzying wave washed over him.

Dylan had to break the silence. "I'm sorry. I know we promised no more secrets."

"You lied to me," Tera said in a flat tone.

"I know. Please don't hate me." Dylan whispered the last part.

"I don't hate you," she said softly. "But I will tell you what I think."

Dylan closed his eyes, waiting for her fury to unleash.

"I think you are the most loyal friend a person could

ever have."

Dylan opened his eyes to see Tera's smiling face.

Chapter Seventeen

Dylan hardly had time to feel relieved that Tera wasn't mad he and Kari had the crystals. He had to figure out how to get the earth crystal from his house back to the hospital. He couldn't ask his mom to drive him all the way home and back again. He paced while thoughts fired through his mind until he thought he had a plan. "I need to make a call."

Dylan dialed his sister's number. "Jordan? It's me. I need you to do a huge favor and not ask questions. It's for EJ."

"Sure. What do you need?" she asked.

"I need you to go into my room and find the Lego house I built that's sitting on my shelf. Inside is a crystal rock. I need you to bring it to the hospital."

"Dylan, I can't. I'm headed to dance practice and it's rehearsal for the state competition. I'm so sorry."

Dylan wanted to throw the phone against the wall, but he blew his frustration out in a big breath. A new idea popped into his head. "Well then can you drop the rock off at Mr. Lyman's house?"

"Yeah, I 'spose. But I have to leave now."

"Okay. Thank you. If he's not home, just put it in his mailbox or something. I'll call him and tell him to look for it."

"Sure thing. Hey, Dylan, how's EJ?"

"Not too good. But I'm hoping things will get better soon."

"You're a good friend. He's lucky to have you." Jordan paused. "I'll get your rock to Mr. Lyman right away."

"Thanks, Jordan." Dylan hung up and dialed Mr. Lyman's number. After four rings an answering machine picked up. Dylan waited for the automated message to play, followed by the beep.

"Mr. Lyman? Hi, it's Dylan Fisher. I'm hoping you can do me a huge favor. My sister, Jordan, is dropping off the earth crystal, the real earth crystal, to your house, and if you don't mind, I need you to bring it up to the hospital. It's for EJ. He's in bad shape, but I think the crystal might be able to help him. If you get this message, you can call me back. Or just come to the hospital. Please. Thanks."

He hung up and looked at the girls' worried expressions. "I'll try calling back in 15 minutes. Maybe he just ran to the store or something."

Mr. Paine and Mrs. Fisher walked down the hallway toward them, and Kari slid her necklace back under her collar.

"We shouldn't stay much longer," Mr. Paine said.

"But we wanted to get him something from the gift shop, right guys?" Kari gave Tera and Dylan frantic looks.

"Um, yeah," Dylan chimed in. "I think I saw something in the window when we walked by that he'd really like."

"What was it?" Mr. Paine's voice was filled with doubt.

Dylan's mind went blank.

"Wasn't it a baseball hat?" Tera said quickly. "You know how EJ loves baseball."

"Yeah, it was." Dylan had no idea if the hospital gift shop even sold baseball hats.

"We'll take the Doyle's their coffee," Mr. Paine said. "But hurry along."

Dylan and the girls hurried down the hall. They didn't say anything until they were in the elevator.

"What if the gift shop doesn't have a baseball hat?" Dylan asked.

"Then we'll get him something else," Kari said. "The point is to stall until Mr. Lyman can get here with the crystal."

"But I have no idea if he'll even get my message!" Dylan got off the elevator when it stopped in the lobby and walked into the nearby gift shop. Not a single baseball hat. "Figures," he muttered.

They wandered around the store, picking up small trinkets and putting them back on the shelves. Dylan rolled his eyes at the wall of stuffed animals—teddy bears wearing "you are beary loved" shirts, gorillas holding satin "I love you" hearts, and dogs with "get well" balloons tied to their tails. EJ would make fun of all of it.

He walked over to Tera who was looking at the flower arrangements. "Flowers would at least brighten his room," she said as she ran her finger along a bright yellow sunflower petal.

Dylan shrugged. "Maybe Mrs. Doyle would like it, but EJ wouldn't care."

"I think he'd like them." Tera didn't seem to be listening.

"This is useless," Dylan said. "I'll be in the lobby." He sulked out of the gift shop and slumped into one of the stiff-backed chairs in the waiting area. He watched the people entering the hospital and wondered how many of them were visiting someone as sick as EJ. Probably none.

Dylan took out his phone and dialed Mr. Lyman's number again. After four rings, the answering machine picked up, but Dylan didn't leave another message. He leaned forward and dropped his head into his hands. He would have to get the crystal here himself.

"Dylan?"

Dylan looked up when he heard the familiar male voice. He almost tackled Mr. Lyman when he hugged him. "You got my message!"

"I did. How is EJ?"

"Unconscious and wrapped up from head to toe," Dylan said.

Mr. Lyman reached into his pocket and pulled out the earth crystal. "I brought what you asked me to, but I'm not sure how you think it's going to help."

Dylan wanted to tell his neighbor everything—all about the crystals, the catalysts, and EJ's power. But he didn't want to take the time. EJ needed his help right away. "I don't either. But I need to try."

Kari and Tera came out of the gift shop and smiled when they saw Mr. Lyman. Kari had the stuffed dog under her arm. "I know it's silly, but the dog's big brown eyes remind me of EJ." She gave it a pat on the head.

"I think he'll like it," Dylan said. "Let's go back up and give him his...gifts."

When they got back to EJ's hospital room, it was

full of all the adults: the Doyle's, Mr. Paine, and Mrs. Fisher.

Mr. Lyman glanced at Dylan and cleared his throat. "I think the kids would like a minute alone with EJ," he said. "It looks like they have a gift for him. Perhaps we could all wait outside?"

"Of course." Mrs. Doyle gave each of the kids a hug before walking out of the room. Dylan gave Mr. Lyman a relieved look as the adults left the room. This was their one chance.

"So what are supposed to do?" Kari asked.

"I'm not sure. Why don't you hold onto the wind crystal, and Tera you take the earth crystal. I'll help EJ hold the fire crystal." Dylan held out the earth crystal for Tera. She just stared at it in his hand. "Come on, now is not the time to be afraid of it."

"But what if...?"

"It has to be buried in the ground after you touch it for anything to happen, and there's no way for it to do that here." Dylan reached out farther toward her.

Tera took the earth crystal, and as soon as her hand touched it, the green center flashed.

"Whoa, mine's glowing too." Kari held out the wind crystal, and its yellow triangle glowed. "It's never been that bright before."

Dylan approached EJ and lifted the edge of the bed sheet, exposing EJ's right hand. He placed it on top of the fire crystal and held it there. A red light radiated between EJ's fingers. "His hand is already getting warm. I don't want it to burn him again."

"I have an idea." Kari closed her eyes. Within seconds Dylan felt a cool breeze above his hand and noticed the bed sheet flapping. It was like a fan blowing right at him.

"Are you doing that?" he asked Kari. She slowly opened her eyes and nodded. "I think it's helping. His hand is cooling off. I can feel it."

"Do you think his burns are healing?" Tera asked.

Dylan found the end of the gauze that wrapped around EJ's hand and carefully peeled it back, revealing EJ's burned fingers. Light from the fire crystal shone under EJ's hand, but oozing blisters still covered his skin. "Nothing's happening."

Tera stepped forward. "I feel like I need to do something to help, but I'm not sure what." She placed her hand on EJ's arm. Suddenly, the red light jumped to where she had touched him.

Dylan flinched. "Did you see that? You made the light move. Do it again."

Tera touched EJ's forehead. This time the red light traveled up EJ's arm, across his shoulder, neck, and cheek until it landed on his forehead.

Dylan smiled at Tera. "It's just like an earthquake spreading across the ground." He unraveled the gauze around EJ's arm up to his elbow. All three of them gasped.

The two places where Tera had touched EJ—the top of his hand and forearm—had smooth, pink, healthy skin. Dylan unraveled the gauze up to EJ's shoulder where the light had traveled. His entire bicep was healed.

"That's it," Dylan whispered. "Kari keeps his skin cool, and Tera moves the light around his body, healing him. We can do it. We can save EJ's life."

Chapter Eighteen

Dylan and the girls worked in silence. Kari kept up a steady airflow to cool off EJ's skin while Tera ran her hands above his body, tracing it with the crystal's red light like a laser pointer. Dylan followed by removing the bandages to reveal patches of delicate, pink skin. It only took them a few minutes to transform his entire body.

Tera stepped away from the bed as though she was admiring her work. "When will he wake up?"

Dylan tucked the blanket around EJ's sides. "Maybe it takes longer for his lungs to heal. Skin is easy."

"Guys, there's just one thing we haven't figured out yet," Kari said. "How are we going to explain how the skin on his entire body healed so suddenly?"

Dylan's high over helping EJ plummeted. He hadn't thought about what they'd tell the doctors and nurses, let alone EJ's parents, or Mr. Paine. Especially Mr. Paine. He was going to suspect something. But it didn't matter. EJ was going to get better. And once everyone saw that, they wouldn't care how it had happened. "We'll just call it a miracle. Nobody can argue that."

As soon as Dylan said the words, the door opened and Mr. Lyman and Mr. Paine walked into the room. Dylan and the girls jumped away from the bed like it shocked them.

"Everything okay in here?" Mr. Paine asked.

"Yep." Dylan stared at the end of the hospital bed to avoid looking him in the eye.

"How's he doing?" Mr. Lyman stepped toward EJ. He leaned over the bed and peered at him like he was examining one of rocks. He adjusted his glasses. "Didn't you say the burns covered his entire body?" he asked over his shoulder.

Mr. Paine nodded. "The doctors said ninety-nine percent burn cover."

"Well it looks to me like he's ninety-nine percent healed."

Dylan's gaze shot toward Mr. Paine to see his reaction.

"What are you talking about?" Tera's dad strode to the bed and ran his hand along one of EJ's uncovered arms. "Impossible," he muttered. He looked around the room at Dylan and the girls, and then addressed Tera. "How did this happen?"

She looked down and rubbed her hands then glanced up at her dad. "I guess it's some sort of miracle," she said.

Mr. Paine stared at her for several seconds. Tera didn't look away. Their eyes locked like two animals in a face-off. Dylan couldn't believe Mr. Paine was the first one to break.

"I'd better go find the doctor." Tera's dad left the room.

Nobody spoke for several seconds. "It's a miracle, indeed." Mr. Lyman broke the silence. "I assume this is what you needed the earth crystal for?"

Dylan nodded. He wanted to tell Mr. Lyman how

they got all three crystals to work together, but he knew Tera and Kari would freak out if he exposed their secret.

"I'm glad you were able to put it to good use." Mr. Lyman smiled. "But you need to get it back into a safe place. When EJ's miraculous recovery gets out to the media, someone on the wrong side might put two and two together and come looking for it."

"You really think someone would come here, to the hospital, looking for the earth crystal?" Dylan asked.

Mr. Lyman nodded. "You need to be extra careful. Now that you know the crystals have additional capabilities, it makes them getting into the wrong hands even more dangerous."

Dylan looked up when Mr. Lyman said "crystals." Did he know they had other crystals? Or was he just assuming all the crystals had healing powers? Before he had a chance to ask, EJ started coughing.

"He's waking up!" Kari said. She, Tera, and Dylan surrounded the bed.

EJ's eyes fluttered opened. He gazed at everyone in the room, staring at each of them for several seconds as though trying to remember who they all were.

"Hey, EJ, we're all here." Tera's voice was just above a whisper. "You're in the hospital, but you're going to be okay."

His eyes locked on Dylan, and one corner of his mouth twitched. Dylan moved closer, leaning in. He thought EJ might be trying to say something.

"Hun...gry," EJ choked out.

A laugh snorted out of Dylan's nose. Leave it to EJ to be on his deathbed and the one thing he was thinking about was food.

"I'll get you anything you want," Dylan said. "Hamburger? Fries? Pizza?"

"Taco...mac." The other side of EJ's mouth curled into a smile.

Dylan wanted to throw his arms around his friend and hug him.

"Did he just say 'taco mac'?" Kari asked. "Whatever it is, it sounds disgusting."

"It's not," Dylan said with a grin. "It's the greatest thing ever."

Mr. Paine and Mrs. Fisher walked back into the room with a doctor and two nurses. EJ's parents were right behind them. Mrs. Doyle hovered over EJ, crying and kissing his face when she saw he was awake.

Mr. Paine motioned to Dylan, Kari, and Tera. "Come on, kids. Let's step out and give everyone else some room."

Once they were in the hallway Dylan wasn't sure what they were supposed to do. He leaned against the wall, letting his head fall back on it. It wasn't even lunch time and he felt like he could crawl back into bed and sleep the rest of the day.

"Does anyone need a ride home?" Mr. Lyman asked.

"I can go with Tera and her dad," Kari said.

Mrs. Fisher looked at her watch. "Would you mind giving Dylan a ride? I need to stop in at work."

"I'd be happy to," Mr. Lyman said.

Dylan didn't care who gave him a ride home. He wanted to leave before people started asking questions about EJ's recovery.

Mr. Doyle stuck his head out of the room. "Dylan, EJ wants to see you."

Kari and Tera's eyes grew wide, and Dylan's heart jumped. This is what he was hoping to avoid. He went back into the room and stood beside EJ's bed.

"Oh, Dylan, it's a miracle, isn't it?" Mrs. Doyle's nose was runny and tears streaked her cheeks. She turned toward the doctor who was telling Mr. Doyle they planned to keep EJ a few more days for observation.

EJ grabbed Dylan's wrist. "Dude, I don't know what you did, but thanks," he whispered.

"Wasn't me. It was the girls. And the…" He glanced at the adults. "Crystals."

"I figured," EJ said. Then he took Dylan's hand and forced something in it—the fire crystal. "Keep it safe until I get out of this joint."

Dylan nodded and slipped the crystal into his pocket.

"Oh, and about the stuffed dog…" EJ said.

"That wasn't me either," Dylan interrupted. "Kari picked it out."

"Tell her thanks. It's better than some stinky flowers." EJ closed his eyes, and Dylan made his way past the adults and left the room.

Kari and Tera huddled around him when he walked out.

"Well?" Kari asked.

"He's gonna be fine. He gave me the fire crystal back. And he said to tell you thanks for the dog. He really liked it."

Kari's face reddened and she broke out into a smile.

Mr. Paine and Mr. Lyman walked toward them, and the kids broke apart from their huddle. "Time to go," he said and strode down the hall. They all quickly followed.

Right before they reached the doors at the end of the

hall, they flew open. Dylan stopped so abruptly he ran into the back of Tera's dad. When he backed up he saw who had come through the doors—Colonel Thornton.

"Richard, I'm so glad you're here," the Colonel said. "Mr. Lyman, nice to see you as well. Hello, kids." He nodded at everyone.

"Colonel, what are you doing here?" Mr. Paine asked as they shook hands.

"Reports of the fire made national news. When I found out it was in your neighborhood I came right away. I trust everyone is okay?" The Colonel looked each of them in the eye.

"Luckily, we all made it out in time." Mr. Paine said.

"Dylan, I understand you were with EJ when it happened," the Colonel said. "Do you have any idea how the fire started?"

Dylan felt his cheeks grow hot. The Colonel looked at him like he already knew the answer and was daring Dylan to lie. *No, he couldn't possibly know about the fire crystal*, Dylan thought. *Could he?*

"Investigators think it must have been kids messing around in the creek with a lighter or something," Mr. Paine said. "Not Dylan and EJ, of course. They were just in the wrong place at the wrong time."

Dylan's mouth dropped open. Mr. Paine knew the truth. He knew about the fire crystal and EJ's power. He was there in the creek with them. So why had he lied to the Colonel?

The two men looked at each other for several seconds. The Colonel seemed to be deciding if he believed Mr. Paine. Finally he spoke again. "And how is EJ doing?"

"His recovery can only be explained as miraculous,"

Mr. Paine said. "I need to get these kids home. It's been a long morning. Feel free to stop by the house before you head back out of town."

"Oh, I'll be here for a few days," the Colonel said. "So I'll be in touch soon." He smiled and went down the hall toward EJ's room.

"Nice of the Colonel to stop by," Mr. Lyman said as they made their way into the elevator.

"Mmmm." Mr. Paine's caterpillar eyebrows were scrunched tight.

"It's interesting he was able to get here so quickly and is taking such an interest in the matter," Mr. Lyman continued.

"Yes, but he is my boss. My business is his business."

"Is that so?" Mr. Lyman glanced at Dylan. Mr. Paine didn't respond. The elevator doors opened and they filed out, walking together through the lobby and into the parking lot.

"I'll call you later," Tera whispered to Dylan. "Bye, Mr. Lyman."

Dylan waved at the girls and went in the opposite direction toward Mr. Lyman's Prius. He shifted in the seat after he buckled. His body felt jittery and uncomfortable, but he couldn't figure out why. He put his hand on his pocket to make sure the fire crystal was still there. It was. The earth crystal was in his other pocket. Even though they were both safe, he couldn't shake off his nerves.

"I meant what I said about protecting the crystal," Mr. Lyman said. "And I get the distinct impression Mr. Paine and Colonel Thornton aren't being honest with each other. I'm just not sure which one is telling the truth."

Dylan stiffened. Mr. Paine was the one lying. Suddenly all of his suspicions about Mr. Paine working for 4E Labs came flooding back. Maybe the Colonel was beginning to suspect the same thing?

"Remember, Dylan. Sometimes those we trust the most are the ones who deceive us the most."

Dylan looked at his elderly neighbor. Mr. Lyman was right. No matter how he felt about Tera, he couldn't let that get in the way of finding out the truth about her dad. And maybe the only way to find out the truth was to finally start telling the truth.

Chapter Nineteen

Three days later EJ was released from the hospital. A giant "Welcome Home" banner hung across the front porch of his house, and rainbow-colored balloons were tied to his mailbox. Dylan, Kari, and Tera sat with EJ in his front living room while a parade of friends and neighbors came through to visit, each bringing a casserole or dessert for the Doyle's.

EJ's skin had healed but was still bright pink, like he had just finished peeling after a bad sunburn. He got around okay, but if he moved too quickly, he'd start coughing. The doctor had said his lungs just needed to get back into shape.

The one question everyone asked was how EJ managed his miraculous recovery? Dylan's heart skipped a beat every time he heard the words. But EJ's standard answer put him at ease:

"You think God was going to let this pitching arm go to waste? Not a chance."

Mrs. Doyle put her hand over her heart whenever EJ said it, which made Dylan smile, even though he knew the real reason behind EJ's recovery.

When the last guest left, Mrs. Doyle brought in a tray with samples of the desserts that everyone had brought. "EJ has the nicest friends, and you all deserve to celebrate."

"Thanks, Mom! You're the best!" EJ lunged for the tray, and Mrs. Doyle managed to kiss the top of his head before leaving them alone with their dessert buffet.

EJ grabbed a handful of cookies and bars and dumped them in his lap. He shoved an entire brownie into his mouth and smiled, his teeth covered in chocolate.

"That's so disgusting," Kari said.

"Yeah, but it's good." EJ wiped his mouth with his sleeve. "Nearly dying has its perks." He ate half a cookie in one bite.

"Don't say that!" Kari scolded. "What if we hadn't been able to save you?"

EJ smirked. "Admit it. You would have missed me."

Kari crossed her arms and leaned back in the recliner. "I would have missed making fun of you and proving you wrong. But I would not have missed having to watch you eat."

"I would have missed you," EJ said to her.

"You would?" Kari's face lit up.

"Sure. I would have missed being able to call you Scary Kari for the rest of my life." EJ held his stomach and faked a laugh.

Kari rolled her eyes. "I think I liked you better when you were in a coma."

EJ ate the other half of his cookie. "So exactly how did you guys figure out how to work your magic on me?"

"We guessed," Dylan said.

"I'm glad you guessed right."

"Seriously, we just took a total stab in the dark and decided to see if the crystals could work together," Dylan said.

EJ had a look on his face like he was concentrating

on a test. "Where did you get the crystals? I thought you only had one. The fire crystal."

Everyone else knew. Dylan decided EJ might as well know too. "I have the earth crystal, and…"

"I have the wind crystal." Kari pulled the necklace out from underneath her hoodie.

It took a minute for the realization to cross EJ's face. "I don't even want to know where you got that. But I do want to know how you made them all work. Here, show me." EJ stuck out his arm.

"We can't show you," Dylan said. "I don't have the earth crystal with me. It's at home. And you're all healed. We can't just make something happen."

"Kari has her crystal." EJ pointed at her. "Have it do something to me."

"I think the smoke has damaged your brain," she said.

EJ stood up and walked over to Kari. He still held out his arm. "I want to see what you did."

"All I did was keep you cool. So the fire crystal didn't burn you again."

"Show me," EJ said.

"I can't."

"We did it all together," Tera pointed out.

"Do it." EJ held his arm right in front of Kari's face.

Dylan reached over and grabbed EJ's arm. "Come on, man."

EJ shrugged him off and held his arm in place. "Show me, Kari."

"No!" Kari reached up to push his arm away, and he grabbed her wrist. The crystal pendant on Kari's necklace flashed, and a spark flew up out of it. "Ow!" She clasped her hand over the side of her neck.

Kari jumped up off the chair. "You burned me! How dare you!"

EJ took a step back. "I did not. You burned yourself. That spark came out of your necklace."

"Yeah, after you got mad and grabbed my arm!" Kari marched over to Tera. "Did it leave a mark?"

Dylan peered over Tera's shoulder. A red blister slashed across Kari's neck.

"It looks like a bad curling iron burn," Tera said.

Kari spun around and walked up to EJ. "This is all your fault." She poked him in the chest. "You and that temper of yours. You need to learn to control it, or you'll end up killing someone."

EJ's face turned pale. He sat down in the recliner. "You're right. I'm sorry. I didn't mean to hurt you. And I didn't mean to start that fire. I'm dangerous even when I don't have that stupid crystal." He bent over and covered his eyes with his hands.

"EJ's right," Tera said. "Not about being dangerous, but about causing that spark when he wasn't even holding the crystal. It's like he transferred his power to the wind crystal."

"That's kind of like what you did with the earth crystal," Dylan said, recalling how Tera had helped spread the fire crystal's healing power around EJ's body. "EJ, see if you can use the wind crystal to heal Kari."

"I can't," EJ mumbled into his hands.

"Sure you can. Instead of getting mad, focus on the wind crystal and staying calm. Just like you did that day in California."

EJ sat up, took off his baseball hat, and ran his hands

through his hair. "Dude, I have no idea how I did that. It was totally random. I can't actually control this… power."

"Sure you can. I saw you do it. Remember the Taco Mac?"

"It's not that easy," EJ said. "I'm not like Kari or Tera. I can't control it. You just saw for yourself. I can't do it when I'm awake or unconscious. You guys had to do it for me."

Kari knelt on the floor in front of EJ. "Please, EJ? For me?" Her voice was almost a whisper.

EJ let out a sigh. "Fine. Anything to get you guys off my back. What do you want me to do?"

Kari held out her necklace. "Focus on the crystal and stay calm. Think about healing the burn on my neck."

EJ looked at the crystal with a scowl.

"You're not even trying," Kari said.

"Just give me a second," EJ snapped.

Dylan and Tera stood behind Kari, watching EJ. He closed his eyes tight, scrunching his cheeks and nose. Then his face muscles seemed to relax, and he opened his eyes again. He stared at Kari's necklace like he was in a trance. Dylan waved slowly, and EJ didn't even glance at his hand.

Nobody spoke for a full minute.

"I don't think it's working," Dylan whispered.

"Shhh," Kari said.

Dylan and Tera exchanged glances. She gave a little shrug.

Another minute passed. EJ hadn't blinked.

"Maybe we should try this another—" Dylan started.

Kari put her hand up. "The crystal is getting warm.

I can feel it."

Dylan leaned over so he could see her necklace. The yellow crystal was glowing. "It's working!"

The crystal grew brighter until it gave off a blinding flash. Dylan blinked to clear the spots from his vision. Kari had gone from a kneeling to a sitting position, as though the flash had knocked her off balance. EJ shook his head like he had just woken up.

"Did it work?" he asked.

Tera knelt down in front of Kari and brushed her hair off her neck. She broke out into a wide smile. "It worked! Look! The burn is totally gone!"

"Really?" EJ stuck his nose inches from Kari's neck. "Holy cats! I did it!"

Dylan peered over EJ's shoulder. There was no sign that Kari had ever been burned.

Kari rubbed her neck. "I knew you could do it. And I bet the more you practice, the easier it'll get."

EJ jumped up. "I'm gonna practice every chance I get."

"Wait a minute," Dylan said. "You can't go around burning people, or yourself, just so you can practice healing them."

"Maybe it works on other things, like sticks," EJ said. "I can try all kinds of stuff!"

Kari stood up and paced in front of the coffee table. "Do you guys realize that we've just proven, for the second time, that the catalysts can control all the crystals? This is huge! We need to get all three crystals together, and have me, Tera, and EJ see what all we can do."

"I don't think that's a good idea," Tera said. "It's too dangerous. We've proven that one too."

"I agree with Tera," Dylan said. "I think we should try to find the fourth crystal before we do anymore experiments."

"That could take forever," Kari said. "We already have three of the four crystals, so I say we start with those."

"This is the only time you will ever hear me say this, but I agree with Kari," EJ said. Kari stood up taller and smiled.

"You actually only have one crystal," Dylan said. "Tera and I have the other two."

"I want mine back," said EJ.

"It's not yours," Dylan said.

"Yes it is. I'm the catalyst. It belongs to me."

Dylan crossed his arms. "I'm not giving it to you."

"Come on, Dylan," Kari said. "EJ has a right to it. Especially after everything he just went through."

"No." Dylan wasn't about to give it up. EJ wasn't even interested in the crystals until now. "It's for your own good. I'm protecting you."

"I can protect myself and anyone else," EJ said. "I just proved that."

"All you proved is that you got lucky. Just like when you healed yourself in California."

EJ sneered. "You know what? I think you're just jealous that we're all catalysts and you're not."

Dylan felt like EJ had just slugged him in the stomach. Nothing hurt more than the truth.

Chapter Twenty

Dylan slumped in his chair at the kitchen table, picking onions out of his chicken fajita. It was normally one of his favorite dinners, but the peppery smell made his stomach queasy.

"Are you feeling okay?" his mom asked.

"Yeah, I'm fine. Just not hungry."

"He probably ate too much at EJ's this afternoon," Jordan said.

Dylan dropped his fork on his plate at the reminder of his fight with EJ. He had stormed out of EJ's house. Dylan thought about texting to apologize at least a hundred times since then. His best friend had almost died. He didn't want to hold a grudge. But EJ's comment about being jealous had hurt. EJ should be the one to apologize first.

"I think it's nice so many people stopped by to see EJ and give the Doyle's food," Mrs. Fisher said.

"There's still a bunch of cars in front of their house," Jordan said.

"They're news vans," said Mr. Fisher. "Word must have gotten out about EJ's story."

Dylan sat up in his chair. "What do you mean by his 'story'?"

Mr. Fisher took a big bite out of his fajita, green and red peppers slipping out onto his plate. "The story about his miraculous recovery. That's the kind of thing reporters will drive across the country to cover. I bet news crews will be parked on our street for days."

Dylan's grudge against EJ had just been replaced by concern. This was the exact type of thing Mr. Lyman had warned him about. "Can they do that? Isn't there some law against sitting out in front of someone's house stalking them?"

"The media seem to get away with just about anything," Mr. Fisher said.

Mrs. Fisher gave him a disapproving look from across the table. "They just want an interview with EJ, and then I'm sure they'll leave the family alone."

"They can't interview EJ!" Dylan said.

His parents and sister stared at him with their mouths open. Mrs. Fisher rested her fork on her plate. "Dylan, what is going on with you? Whatever it is, we can talk about it."

This was not something he could talk about with his family. There was no way to explain how EJ had recovered from his burns without exposing the secret about the crystals. And even without mentioning it, 4E Labs might still be suspicious. If Mr. Paine and Colonel Thornton really were working for them, then 4E probably already had an idea that something was up. The only way to make sure the secret stayed safe was to stop EJ from doing any interviews.

"Son, you know you can tell us anything," Mr. Fisher said.

Dylan tried to think of something that sounded believable. "EJ's been through a ton already. And you know how news people like to make bigger deals out of things than they need to be. I just don't want them making him out to be some sort of freak."

Mrs. Fisher smiled. "I think it's very sweet that you're so concerned about him. And I bet it'd mean a lot to him to hear you say all that. It might even help him in dealing with all that press."

Dylan knew how stubborn EJ could be, but he had to try and stop him. "May I be excused to go down to EJ's?"

"Yes," Mrs. Fisher said as Dylan jumped up from the table. "But clear your plate first!" He took a few steps, and then slid back in his sock-covered feet to scoop up his plate and cup and dump them in the kitchen sink with a clatter.

Dylan ran to the front door, slipped on his shoes, and went out onto the porch. Two white vans were parked in front EJ's house. Dylan shuddered at the memory of Frank and the white van used to kidnap Tera. But these vans were clearly marked with local news station logos. Still, he couldn't calm what felt like grasshoppers jumping in his stomach.

Dylan let out a deep breath and walked across the street to EJ's house. When he passed the first news van, a guy with a beard and backwards baseball hat sat up in the driver's seat. He didn't get out of the van, but Dylan could feel the guy watching every step he took toward EJ's front door. After he rang the bell, he glanced behind him. The guy stared right at him. Dylan quickly turned back around.

He heard a lot of voices coming from inside the house. Finally the front door opened, and all of the Doyle's stood crowded together in the entryway. They all talked at once over each other, and nobody seemed to notice Dylan. Except for EJ.

"What are you doing here?" EJ said with disdain.

"Um, I was just coming to talk to you," Dylan muttered.

"Well your timing couldn't be worse. I'm headed to greet my fans." EJ nodded toward the news vans.

"Your *fans*?" Dylan asked.

"Yeah. They've been waiting for me all day. The reporter said half the country has already heard about me, and I can't disappoint all the people who want to hear my story."

EJ sounded like a total diva. He pushed past Dylan, and his family hurried out behind him like some sort of entourage.

"EJ, wait! I need to talk to you before you talk to the press." Dylan reached for EJ's arm to stop him.

"Let go of me!" EJ shook him off.

"Come on, this is important, and it'll only take a sec."

EJ spun around to face Dylan. "I don't have time, Dylan. This is more important anyway." He turned and caught up to his family who were gathered around the reporter and cameraman.

Dylan stood in the middle of EJ's yard. He'd never heard EJ call him by his first name. He had called him 'Fish' as long as he could remember. There was nothing Dylan could do now. He had to just hope that EJ wouldn't say the wrong thing.

A woman with blond hair curled perfectly at the ends stood holding a microphone. Her long red coat fit snug around her waist. Dylan recognized her from TV, but she looked shorter in person. The guy from the front seat of the van held a video camera on one shoulder. Another guy was attaching a tiny microphone onto EJ's hoodie.

The Doyle's chattered with excitement, and Dylan stood a few feet behind them. EJ glanced at him once and glared.

"Okay, EJ, I'm just going to ask you a few questions about what happened the day of the fire," the reporter said. "Think of it as a regular conversation. Pay no attention to the camera. Say whatever comes to mind, and we can stop at any time if you need to."

"I got this," EJ said.

Dylan inched closer and stood beside Mr. and Mrs. Doyle. The guy in the baseball hat hoisted the camera onto his shoulder. The reporter straightened her coat, held the microphone underneath her chin, and plastered a big fake smile across her face. The camera man gave her a thumbs up.

"This is Veronica Baker, and I'm standing outside the home of EJ Doyle, the young man who just a few days ago was caught in a forest fire that burned 90 percent of his body. Yet somehow, EJ's body healed itself in just 24 hours. Doctors have no explanation, other than to call it a miracle." She turned toward EJ. "How are you feeling just days after this terrible accident?"

"I feel awesome," EJ said. "Like a whole new person."

"You look amazing," Veronica said. "Do you remember what happened that day in the forest behind your neighborhood?"

Dylan leaned forward to make sure he could hear EJ's response.

"Not really. My...neighbor and I were hanging out by the creek, and all of a sudden we smelled smoke. Then the trees all started catching fire. After that, I don't remember much."

Neighbor? EJ hadn't even bothered to call Dylan his friend. He was madder than Dylan thought.

"Is that the neighbor you were with?" Veronica nodded toward Dylan.

EJ looked at him and gave a scowl. "Yeah, that's Dylan."

The camera man motioned for Dylan to come forward. Dylan shook his head. He didn't want to be on camera. And he was pretty sure EJ didn't want him to either.

"Go on, Dylan," Mr. Doyle said.

Dylan reluctantly walked up and stood beside EJ.

"Can you tell us what happened in the creek?" Veronica asked.

Dylan stared into the dark camera lens. It was like a black hole. He blinked and tried to think of what to say. "It's like EJ said. The fire just kind of came out of nowhere. We ran out but then thought someone else was trapped in it, so we went back. I found my way out again, but EJ didn't."

"So there was someone else in the creek with you?" Veronica's words came out faster this time.

Dylan realized his mistake. "Uh, no, not with us. Maybe it was the one who started the fire or something. We never actually saw anyone else." His heart pounded in his chest so loudly, he thought the reporter could have heard it.

"Investigators haven't determined a cause yet for

the fire, but arson is suspected."

Was she accusing them? Dylan stared at the sidewalk and didn't look at her.

"Doctors are calling this the Mile High Miracle," Veronica changed the subject. "EJ, do you agree?"

"I guess so. I've always been able to heal fast. Maybe it's just good genes."

"The doctors and nurses as Castle Pines Hospital were amazing," Mrs. Doyle added off camera.

"Speaking of that, I have some exciting news that we just learned." Veronica reached into her coat pocket and unfolded a piece of paper. "A donation has been made to the Castle Pines Hospital burn unit in EJ's name, in the amount of $10,000."

EJ's parents gasped.

"It was?" EJ said. "Who would do that?"

Veronica held the microphone closer to her mouth and smiled. "4E Labs."

Chapter Twenty-One

EJ gave Dylan a horrified look at the mention of 4E Labs. Veronica held the microphone in front of EJ, waiting for his response. After several seconds, Mrs. Doyle stepped forward and took over.

"How wonderful!" She clapped her hands together. "What a generous donation! We are so grateful for everything this community has done to support EJ and our entire family."

Dylan tuned out the rest of the interview. His mind raced trying to make sense of things. There was no way the donation could be a random coincidence. 4E Labs must be trying to send a message. And that message had to be that they knew about EJ and the fire crystal. But how?

Across the street Tera's garage door opened, and Mr. Paine's black Hummer SUV pulled out of the driveway. That was the only explanation. Mr. Paine must have told 4E. And maybe they thought that by making a donation to the hospital, they would have a reason to contact EJ and try to sniff out any information they could about the crystal. Or figure out how to get the crystal from him. Which meant it was more important than ever that Dylan hang onto the crystal and not give it to EJ. Especially after this latest move by 4E. Dylan was pretty sure that just based off the look on EJ's face, he wouldn't argue about Dylan keeping the crystal for now.

The interview ended, and the camera guy quickly packed up the van.

"When will this air?" Mrs. Doyle asked.

Veronica looked at her watch. "On the ten o'clock news if we're lucky." She turned toward EJ. "Thank you. That was perfect. By this time tomorrow you'll be famous! I wouldn't be surprised if it goes viral."

EJ gave her a weak smile and then motioned for Dylan to follow him inside. Neither one said anything until they were in EJ's room with the door closed.

"Dude…" EJ said.

"I know." Dylan paced in front of EJ's bed. The fact EJ was talking to him again was overshadowed by this bigger issue.

"How does 4E Labs know about me?"

Dylan couldn't keep the secret about Mr. Paine from EJ. Not anymore. "I think Tera's dad and Colonel Thornton might be secretly working for them."

EJ dropped into his bean bag chair on the floor. "What? No way! Does Tera know?"

"I tried telling her, but she doesn't believe me. I don't have enough proof."

"Well find some! I don't want Mr. Paine, Colonel Sanders, or the creepy lab guys coming after me!"

Dylan stopped pacing. "That's the part I don't know how to do. If Tera doesn't believe me then she won't help me prove her dad is guilty. And I can't just go up and ask him or the colonel. They'll both deny it. And if I ask Jessica about it, she'll just tell Mr. Paine. I need to find someone else who knows about the crystals, and who also knows about 4E Labs. Frank would have been a good one, but he's a dead end. Literally."

EJ threw a balled up sock at Dylan's face.

"Hey, what was that for?"

"Do I really have to spell this one out for you?" EJ asked.

Dylan had no idea what EJ meant.

"You need someone who knows about the crystals and knows about 4E, right?"

Dylan looked at EJ, but his mind drew a blank.

"Dude, what about your geocaching buddy?"

Realization finally dawned on Dylan. "Are you talking about Mr. Lyman?"

EJ nodded.

Why hadn't Dylan thought of him? That was perfect! Not only did Mr. Lyman know about most of it, but he was also a stockholder of 4E Labs. Maybe he knew someone who worked there? Dylan had never thought to ask him. But now he would. "You're a genius!"

EJ gloated. "Does this mean I get the fire crystal?"

Dylan froze. They had just started talking again. He didn't want to get into another fight.

"Just kidding," EJ said. "I don't want that thing anywhere near me, especially if the enemy comes knocking!"

Dylan wiped a drip of sweat from his temple in relief.

"Wanna stay and watch my big debut on TV?"

It would be at least an hour before the news came on, and Dylan needed to figure out his plan for talking to Mr. Lyman the next day. He also didn't think he could handle hearing about EJ's story and listening to a replay about the latest development with 4E Labs. "I should probably get home."

"Okay. But let me know how it goes with the old man."

Dylan walked himself out and went home. He headed straight to his room. He didn't bother waiting for the news to come on TV. It would be all over the Internet. Where anyone could see it.

***

When Dylan woke up the next morning, his family was already buzzing about the interview. Dylan slid into his chair at the kitchen table and took a long sip of orange juice.

"EJ did a wonderful job," Mrs. Fisher said. "And you got on camera! I recorded the whole thing if you want to watch it after breakfast."

"I was standing right there, Mom." Dylan poured some frosted Rice Krispies into the bowl in front of him.

"And that donation to the hospital! Such a nice gesture from that company." Mrs. Fisher stood at the sink drinking her coffee.

Dylan groaned to himself and took a bite. The sweet rice tingled and popped in his mouth.

Mr. Fisher sat back at the end of the table, finished with his usual two fried eggs and two strips of bacon. "What's on the agenda today, Dylan? More geocaching?"

"I don't know. Maybe. I need to go talk to Mr. Lyman." He knew his parents would assume he wanted to talk to him about geocaching.

"Will you please invite him over for dinner?" Mrs. Fisher said. "I feel bad he doesn't have anybody to cook for him, and he's always alone in that empty house. I'll even make a pie if it'll entice him."

"He's not alone," Jordan said. "I see some green car in his driveway all the time. Probably his girlfriend." She snickered over her own bowl of Rice Krispies.

Dylan wrinkled his nose at the thought of Mr. Lyman having a girlfriend. Wasn't he too old? And he never mentioned going out anywhere. It didn't matter. Dylan had more important things to talk to Mr. Lyman about.

After breakfast Dylan walked down the street to his neighbor's house. It was hard to believe it was the beginning of January and he was warm in his hoodie. School would be starting back up in a few days, but it seemed like it should be summer break.

There weren't any unfamiliar cars in Mr. Lyman's driveway. Dylan rang the doorbell and waited. He smiled when he saw the old man's friendly, blue eyes.

"Good morning, Dylan! What brings you all this way at this hour? Shouldn't you be sleeping in?" Mr. Lyman held the door open so Dylan could come inside.

The aroma of coffee hit Dylan's nose. It always smelled a little burned, like it had been on too long. But the smell comforted Dylan, along with the dimly lit living room and white lace curtains over the kitchen windows that blew in the breeze whenever Mr. Lyman had the windows open, like he did today.

"Lemonade?" Mr. Lyman asked.

"Yes, please." Dylan never turned down a glass of Mr. Lyman's fresh-squeezed lemonade. He sat down in the green vinyl chair at the kitchen table as Mr. Lyman pulled a glass from the cabinet.

"I saw EJ's interview on TV last night. Very

impressive." Mr. Lyman pried cubes out of an ice tray. They clinked as he dropped them one at a time into the glass. "Especially the part about 4E Labs." He poured the lemonade and set the glass in front of Dylan, then sat in the chair across the table.

Dylan took a drink and licked the sweet lemonade from his top lip. "That's what I came here to talk to you about."

"The interview or 4E Labs?" Mr. Lyman took a sip of his coffee.

"4E Labs. And what you know about them. Or, who you know there." Dylan always felt comfortable talking to Mr. Lyman, but his hands shook a little as he waited for a response.

Mr. Lyman's eyes squinted slightly. "As a geologist, I believe in doing anything possible to protect our earth. 4E Labs has done a lot to make products that are eco-friendly and help scientists do much needed research; such as earthquake prediction equipment, state-of-the-art solar panels, and new ways to harness wind power. That's why I've been a shareholder of theirs for so long."

"But if you're a shareholder, then don't you make money when they do?" Dylan thought back to Colonel Thornton's comment.

"In theory. But that's not why I invest in the company. I invest because I believe in them and what they're doing."

"So you don't think they're corrupt?" Dylan asked.

Mr. Lyman looked surprised. "Corrupt? Heavens no. Lloyd Stanoshek has been the CEO of 4E Labs for over a decade. I've met him personally a number of times, and he is as honest as they come."

"What about their researchers? Do you know any of them?"

"Dylan, why all these questions? What are you getting at?"

Dylan had never told Mr. Lyman about 4E Labs' involvement in the crystals. But he might as well now. He knew about everything else. Well, except the part about the catalysts. "I think someone from 4E Labs is after the crystals and wants them for their power to make the Creation Stone." He studied Mr. Lyman's face for his reaction, which was blank for several seconds.

"Knowing you, Dylan, you wouldn't come to that conclusion without some pretty concrete evidence. If it's true, it's not anyone at the top of the company. But it's a pretty large corporation, and researchers can be eccentric, even radical types. I'm also assuming that EJ's recovery had something to do with the crystals, which is why you had me bring the earth crystal to the hospital. And I'm sure the donation by 4E Labs has contributed to your suspicions." Mr. Lyman paused and took another sip of coffee. "I promised I would do anything to help you find all four elemental crystals. And if someone is after them, whether connected to 4E Labs or not, I promise to help you find them as well."

Dylan relaxed back into the chair, relieved Mr. Lyman believed him. He didn't know how Mr. Lyman could help, but he knew that he would.

Finally. Someone Dylan could trust.

Chapter Twenty-two

With Mr. Lyman on his side, Dylan could only think of one thing left he needed to do: confront Mr. Paine. Otherwise he'd never find out the truth: whether or not Tera's dad was somehow working with 4E Labs. But he had to figure out how to do that without Tera knowing. She was mad enough when he mentioned it to her. If she found out he wanted to confront her dad directly she'd have a full on, five-alarm freak out.

On his way back home from Mr. Lyman's, Dylan saw Kari in her driveway. She waved, and he walked over.

"What's up?" he asked.

"Just going to see how EJ is doing today after his big TV debut," she said. "What about you?"

"Just ran down to talk to Mr. Lyman." Dylan didn't bother telling her why.

"More geocaching?"

Dylan hadn't done any since they got back from California. He was overdue. "Maybe." He glanced at Tera's house across the street. "Have you talked to Tera?"

"Yes, and she's still waiting for you to apologize for accusing her dad of being a spy."

"But it's true!" Dylan said. "Or at least I think it's true."

Kari gave him a disbelieving look. "Either way, you

should still apologize."

Dylan should have known Tera would tell Kari. "Fine." Right after he found out if her dad really was a spy.

"Do it before tonight," Kari said. "She's spending the night at my house, and I don't need her pouting about her boyfriend."

Dylan stared at Kari, confused.

"I'm talking about YOU, dummy! Apologize so I don't have to hear about how frustrated she is over you all night."

"I'm not her boyfriend." Dylan didn't even know if he was old enough to have a girlfriend. But if he was, Tera would be his first and only choice.

Kari crossed her arms and rolled her eyes. "Okay, okay," Dylan said. He didn't need Kari mad at him too. And if Tera was going to be at Kari's overnight, then that meant Mr. Paine would be home by himself. The perfect time to try and talk to him. "I'll go over to Tera's right now and apologize."

"Good."

Dylan huffed at Kari's big, satisfied smile. He turned and walked back across the street to Tera's house. He wanted to make this quick so he could go home and focus on what to say to Mr. Paine later.

After ringing the doorbell, it was only seconds before Tera answered. She didn't frown when she saw Dylan, but she didn't greet him with her usual warm smile either.

"Hey," she said flatly.

"Hey. Do you have a second?"

Tera came out onto the porch. She wore black

leggings and a t-shirt. Even without shoes on she was still way taller than Dylan.

"I'm sorry for what I said about your dad. About accusing him."

Tera looked at him like she was expecting him to say more. "Ok."

Dylan chewed on the inside of his cheek. "I didn't mean to make you mad."

"Ok."

"So I wanted to apologize," Dylan said.

"You already said that."

Why was Tera making this so hard? Couldn't she just forgive him? "Oh. Yeah. Well, I'm sorry, again."

Tera stared at him for several seconds. Heat built underneath Dylan's hoodie, and it felt tight around his neck. What else did she want him to say?

Then Tera giggled.

Dylan frowned at her. "Why are you laughing?"

"You should see the confused look on your face."

Now he was even more confused.

"I'm just messing with you." Tera grinned. "Thanks for apologizing. I don't like being mad at you." She leaned forward and hugged Dylan. Her long hair tickled his nose. He closed his eyes and inhaled her pine-scented shampoo. She pulled away too soon.

"Whose car is that?" Tera pointed down the street. Dylan turned and saw a green car in Mr. Lyman's driveway that hadn't been there earlier.

"My sister thinks Mr. Lyman has a girlfriend," Dylan said. Mr. Lyman hadn't said anything about someone coming over when Dylan was there, but maybe it was a surprise visit.

"We should go meet her," Tera said.

"What? No way." Dylan didn't want to see old people holding hands. Or worse, kissing. "It might not even be a woman. Could just be a geologist friend or something."

"I hope it's a girlfriend. He needs someone so he's not lonely. Everyone needs someone." She smiled at Dylan, and he felt himself grin back. "I'm sleeping over at Kari's tonight, but we should all hang out tomorrow. It's our last day before school starts again on Monday." She turned to go inside then looked back at him. "And thanks again for apologizing. Twice."

Dylan laughed. "See ya." He stepped off the porch and looked down the street toward Mr. Lyman's house again. Who could be at his house? He was tempted to go back down and find out, but he had just been there. And it wasn't any of his business anyway.

Dylan went home and up to his room. The photo of him and Tera from the overlook was pinned to his bulletin board, and he smiled every time he looked at it. He took the roof off the Lego house that sat on his dresser and peered inside. The earth and fire crystals sat nestled together, almost fitting like puzzle pieces. Both centers gave off a slight glow—one green and one orange-red. He wondered if it was ok for them to be touching each other, or would some sort of reaction happen? But if nothing had happened yet, it probably wouldn't. Dylan reached in and rubbed his finger against each one. Neither one felt warm, like they did when they were activated by a catalyst. And he obviously wasn't a catalyst. Dylan replaced the roof to the Lego house. He wasn't going to focus on that right now. He had to figure out what he was going to say to Mr. Paine.

***

Late in the afternoon the doorbell rang. Dylan answered and greeted Mr. Lyman. He forgot he had invited him to dinner that night, like his mom had asked.

"Hello, Dylan, nice to see you again." Mr. Lyman straightened his glasses on his nose.

"Hi, Mr. Lyman." Dylan glanced behind his neighbor. "Are you here by yourself?"

"Was I supposed to bring a date?" Mr. Lyman chuckled.

Dylan wanted to ask about the green car in Mr. Lyman's driveway, but he chickened out.

"May I come inside?" Mr. Lyman asked. "Something smells awfully good in there."

Dylan held the door open wide for Mr. Lyman, then followed him into the kitchen. Mr. Lyman sat down at the table and chatted with Dylan's parents until dinner was ready. Dylan decided next time he saw the green car parked in Mr. Lyman's driveway, he was going to go down and find out who it was.

Dylan ate his stew quickly and started to fidget while waiting for Mr. Lyman to finish. Why did older people take so long to eat?

"Mom, may I please be excused?" Dylan finally asked.

"Do you have someplace you need to be?" Mrs. Fisher asked.

"I want to see how EJ's doing." Dylan knew his mom couldn't say no to that. And he did plan to stop by

EJ's after talking to Mr. Paine.

"Don't keep him here on my account," Mr. Lyman said to Mrs. Fisher. Then he addressed Dylan. "Tell Egan hello for me."

Dylan looked at his mom. "Oh, all right," she said.

Dylan got up from the table and cleared his plate. "Bye, Mr. Lyman. Good dinner, Mom!"

He went outside onto the front porch and looked up and down the street. A dull hum of distant cars filled the crisp, winter night air. Outdoor lights shone from most of his neighbor's houses. Otherwise the neighborhood was still.

Dylan jogged across the yard to Tera's house. Her porch light was on. She should be at Kari's by now. He rang the doorbell without hesitating. He had decided he was just going to admit to Mr. Paine that he had overheard the phone conversation in the garage. Honesty was usually the best policy.

Finally the door opened, and Mr. Paine filled the doorway. Dylan almost didn't recognize him. Instead of his usual khaki pants and crisp white shirt, he wore athletic pants, a black long-sleeved t-shirt, and a black baseball hat.

"Hi, Dylan. Tera isn't here. She's spending the night at Kari's."

"I know. I came to talk to you." Nervous tingles ran up Dylan's arms like little spiders.

Mr. Paine didn't move, his entire body blocking the entrance. "Oh? What about?"

Dylan swallowed hard. "About something I overheard. When we were in California."

"Are you referring to the phone conversation you

heard while hiding in the garage?"

Guilty heat spread over Dylan's face. He nodded.

Mr. Paine stood silent for several seconds. He stepped to the side, and with his body no longer blocking the doorway, a flood of light from inside the house shone in Dylan's face, making him squint.

"Come inside." Mr. Paine's voice echoed off the entryway. "I think it's time we told each other the truth."

Chapter Twenty-three

Dylan followed Mr. Paine into the kitchen and sat down at the small table, his arms and legs shaking slightly from nerves. He fidgeted with the edge of the placemat, waiting for Mr. Paine to talk first.

"So what do you want to ask me?" Mr. Paine said.

Dylan sat up a little in his chair trying to stir up some confidence. He needed to spit it out. This was it. Now or never. "Are you and Colonel Thornton secretly working for 4E Labs?"

Mr. Paine looked surprised. "Of course not. What would make you think that?"

"On the phone in California, in the garage when you were talking to the colonel, it sounded like you were working for them. You said you wanted to take the fire crystal to the lab."

"I wasn't talking about 4E Labs, Dylan. I was referring to the lab we have within the military."

"But you said you didn't trust anyone there."

"I don't. I prefer to do all testing myself, especially when it comes to the crystals. I always have."

Dylan stared at a thread unraveling on the placemat. "Then why did you lie to the colonel? You said you'd meet him and give him the crystal, but you didn't. You met with Jessica instead."

Mr. Paine sat with his elbows on the table, hands

clenched in front of his chin. Then he sat back into a more relaxed position. "Dylan, in my line of work, one of the first things you learn is to never assume. By that I mean, never assume people are who they appear to be, and never assume people are honest one hundred percent of the time. Because very few people are that way."

Dylan wasn't sure what Mr. Paine was getting at. "So you think all people are phonies and liars?"

"No, not all people. And not all the time. But even the most honest people can withhold information, or phrase it in a way that might not be completely truthful. And everybody pretends to be something they're not at times."

"So are you saying you don't trust Colonel Thornton?" Dylan asked.

"It's not that I don't trust him, but I do know he has certain interests. I have my own interests, and you do too."

Now Dylan was really confused. "I do? What are my interests?"

"You want to protect your friends, no matter what it takes."

That was definitely true. Enough bad things had already happened to them: Tera, EJ, and even Mr. Lyman. If 4E Labs got a hold of the crystals, it would only get worse. "What are your interests?"

"The same as yours. To protect Tera, EJ, Kari, and you." Mr. Paine's voice softened.

"So then what are the colonel's interests? Doesn't he want to protect us too?"

Mr. Paine nodded. "He does, but his interests go far beyond that. He wants to protect the entire country, especially if 4E Labs could potentially threaten the nation as a whole. And if protecting the country requires involving you kids in some way, he won't hesitate to do it. Which is where I step in."

Suddenly Dylan didn't like the colonel anymore. "Then why do you tell the colonel stuff? You didn't have to tell him you had the fire crystal at all."

"Because I need his help and the help of the military to bring down 4E Labs. I can't do it on my own. And until we stop them you kids will never be truly safe. But I can't protect you unless I have all the information. Which is why I need you to tell me the truth about EJ."

Dylan stiffened. He knew coming clean was the right thing to do, but he had spent so much time keeping his friends' secrets, it was hard to finally tell the truth. Mr. Paine had been honest, so it was only fair that Dylan be honest too. "EJ's the catalyst for the fire crystal. But the way it works is weird. Totally different than Tera. The crystal burns EJ, and anyone else, when he's holding it and is mad. But then if he stays calm, he can actually use it to heal. That's how he recovered from his burns. We used it to heal him." Dylan felt lighter with every word and relaxed a little in his chair.

Mr. Paine leaned forward. "We?"

Oops. Dylan hadn't meant to say that much. But it was too late now. "Actually it was just Tera…and Kari."

"Kari?"

"Yeah. She's the catalyst for the wind crystal. Which she has. And I have the real earth crystal. The one you have is a fake."

Mr. Paine stood up. Dylan felt a flicker of fear. Was he in trouble? Mr. Paine paced in front of the table, so

Dylan kept going. "Tera used her power to pull the fire crystal's power through EJ's body, and Kari used hers to keep EJ cool. She can pretty much control any type of wind. Even tornadoes. I didn't really do anything except make sure EJ held onto the crystal since he was unconscious. Somehow it just all worked." Dylan watched Mr. Paine continue to pace for several more minutes before he finally stopped and faced Dylan.

"So you have three of the four crystals, and three of the four catalysts?"

Dylan nodded. "Yeah."

"Does anyone else know all this?" Mr. Paine's eyes focused on Dylan like lasers.

Beads of sweat formed on Dylan's forehead. Maybe he had said too much? "No. Not really."

"What do you mean 'not really?'"

Dylan's stomach squirmed. Had he done something wrong? "Mr. Lyman knows about the crystals, but he doesn't know about the catalysts or how they work."

Mr. Paine closed his eyes and grimaced as though he had a headache. "I know Mr. Lyman is a kind, elderly gentleman, but he has ties to 4E."

Was Mr. Paine accusing Mr. Lyman of being one of the bad guys? Dylan had to set him straight. "I know. But he said if 4E is involved, it's not any of the people in charge of the company. He knows the CEO and says he's a good guy. Mr. Lyman even said he'd help figure out who the bad guy is."

Mr. Paine gave Dylan a look of pity. "Dylan, I like Mr. Lyman, I really do, but as I explained earlier, people tell you what they want you to know."

This was ridiculous. Mr. Lyman had nothing to do

with the enemy. And Dylan would figure out a way to prove it to Mr. Paine. He would trust Mr. Lyman any day. He'd trust him way more than Colonel Thornton. "So how much does the colonel know?"

"Colonel Thornton is my boss, so he has a right to know what's going on. But even he doesn't know about the catalysts."

A wave of relief spread over Dylan. If the colonel knew about the catalysts there was no telling what he might do, especially if he thought it would protect the country.

"Other than Mr. Lyman, does anyone else know?" Mr. Paine asked.

"Jessica knows," Dylan pointed out. "And she's not who she says she is. She's pretending to work for 4E Labs."

"That's different." Mr. Paine sat back down. "She's working undercover to try and figure out why 4E Labs wants the crystals. You know that."

"If you're going to worry about anyone it should be her. Even her red hair looks fake." Dylan thought about the couple of times he had run into her. She twisted his words around and never seemed totally honest.

"I've known Jessica a very long time, and I trust her more than anybody," Mr. Paine said.

"Why? Wouldn't she fall into the same category of only saying what she wants you to know?" Dylan knew he was being mouthy, but he couldn't help it.

"No, she doesn't fall into that category. She tells me everything. And I tell her everything too."

"But how do you know you can trust her? She uses code names like Mile High. And Tera isn't even allowed to meet with her in person. What's that all about?" Dylan heard the snippiness in his voice, but he didn't care.

"Again, it's to protect Tera." Mr. Paine really annunciated the "T" in her name. "Because Jessica works at 4E, we have to be extra careful when it comes to Tera."

"Exactly. And of all the people you say you can trust the most, it's someone who works at 4E! And what has she found out? Nothing. Either she's bad at her job, or she's lying about what she knows."

"She's not lying. And that's all I'm going to say about Jessica." Mr. Paine's voice rose slightly.

Dylan couldn't let it go. He was too stirred up inside. "If you trust her so much, then let Tera meet her."

"Absolutely not," Mr. Paine said.

"Why not? If she is who she says, and she's the most honest person you know, then there shouldn't be a problem." Dylan didn't know where the defiance was coming from, but it felt good.

"Tera is not going to meet Jessica, and that's final!" Mr. Paine's loud voice echoed in the kitchen.

Dylan slammed his palms down on the table. "Why not? Give me one good reason!"

Mr. Paine stood up, knocking his chair over. "Because she's my wife!"

Dylan took a second for the words to sink in. Mr. Paine's wife? "When did you get remarried?" he asked, completely confused.

"He didn't." Tera stood in the doorway between the front hall and kitchen. Dylan wondered how long she had been there.

"Tera…" Mr. Paine's stern expression turned to

surprise.

"Is Jessica my mother?" Tera asked quietly.

Dylan froze, the meaning of Mr. Paine's words finally sinking in. He stared at Tera's dad, waiting for an answer.

Mr. Paine stood like a soldier at attention. Then his shoulders slumped. "Yes."

Chapter Twenty-four

The only sound in the kitchen for several minutes was the clock ticking on the wall. Why wasn't Tera freaking out? Her mother was alive! Dylan couldn't stand the tension. He had to say something.

"What are *you* doing here?" he blurted.

Tera didn't turn her attention away from her dad. "I stopped home to grab my toothbrush." She finally looked at Dylan, and her eyes narrowed, forming a deep crease between them that he had never seen before. "What are you doing here?"

Dylan wasn't prepared for that question. "I, I was telling your dad about how we healed EJ."

"Did you know Jessica was really my mother?" The crease between Tera's eyes softened, but her expression looked hurt and her voice quivered.

Dylan shook his head until he was almost dizzy. "No! I had no idea until now." And he could hardly believe it. He had met Tera's mother before Tera had met her.

"Tera, let me explain," Mr. Paine said.

"Do not tell me you've been lying to me all these years just to protect me!" Tera said.

Mr. Paine closed his mouth.

"I've got news for you, Dad. I don't need protecting. What I need is a mother! She'd be a way better parent than you!" Raindrop-sized tears streamed down Tera's cheeks.

Dylan wanted to crawl underneath the table. He didn't want to watch Tera and her dad argue. Mr. Paine's eyes looked watery. Was he going to cry too?

"Tera, I don't blame you for being mad or feeling like you hate me right now. And I promise you will be reunited with your mother. But not right now. She and I both agree on that. We're getting closer to figuring out this whole thing with 4E Labs, and as soon as we know it's safe—".

"I want to see her! Now!" Tera stomped her foot, and Dylan cringed at the vibration it made in the room. But he didn't blame her. He'd want to punch the wall if he were her.

"Dylan, do you mind?" Mr. Paine said. "This is family business."

"Sure. I can let myself out." Dylan stood up and headed toward the door. Tera grabbed his arm as he walked by.

"Sorry. I'll call you."

"Good luck," he mumbled. When he got outside, the chilly night air felt soothing. His heart raced as he hurried across the street to Kari's house. Had all that really just happened? His mind and body felt disconnected, like he was daydreaming. He must have rang Kari's doorbell because the next thing he realized she answered.

"I thought you'd be Tera," Kari said. "She ran home to get her toothbrush and isn't back yet."

"I know. I was just over there. Major news." Dylan could hardly form sentences.

Kari came out onto the porch. "What's going on? Are you okay? You look like you could hurl."

Dylan shook his head and tried to focus. "You know Jessica? She's really Tera's mom."

Kari gasped. "As in Tera's *dead* mom?"

Dylan nodded. "But she's not dead. Never was."

"Is Tera freaking out?"

"Pretty much. She demanded to see her mom, but her dad said as long as 4E Labs is after the crystal, Jessica needs to lay low."

Kari pulled at the necklace around her neck. "This is huge! I can't imagine thinking my mom has been dead for years and then finding out she's just been in hiding. Does EJ know?"

"Not yet. It all just happened." Dylan still felt like he was dreaming.

"We need to tell him. Come on." Kari started walking toward EJ's house next door.

At first Dylan wasn't sure they needed to tell EJ that minute. But he quickly dismissed it. No more lies. Not about anything or for anybody.

Kari had already rung the doorbell by the time Dylan joined her on EJ's front porch. Mr. Doyle answered the door and called for EJ to come downstairs.

EJ's hair stuck up in all directions like he had just woken up. "Hey guys, what's up?"

"We have big news." Kari motioned for them to go back outside.

"Bigger than me being on TV?" EJ asked.

Kari glared at him. "Way bigger. We found out Tera's mom is really alive. And it's Jessica."

EJ looked back and forth at Kari and Dylan. "What? I knew there was something not right about her. She's back from the dead like a zombie!"

"She's not a zombie," Dylan said, annoyed that EJ wasn't taking it seriously. "But she is working undercover at 4E Labs. And Mr. Paine is not the enemy. He's trying to figure out this whole 4E Labs thing too."

"It would have been better if she had been a zombie," EJ muttered. "What about old Mr. Lysol down the street? What'd you find out about him?"

"Mr. Lyman is a good guy too," Dylan said. "They're all trying to help."

"Then what's the big deal?"

Dylan got so frustrated when EJ didn't seem to understand things. "The big deal is that whatever is going on with the crystals is big enough for Mr. Paine to lie about Tera's mom being dead all these years."

EJ frowned. "Well, what are we supposed to do about it?"

"I'm not sure yet," Dylan said. "But I'm going to figure it out."

"Let me know when you do. And if you need me to burn some zombies, you know where to find me." EJ winked and went back inside.

"Moron," Kari muttered on the way back to her house. She stopped in her driveway and stared across the street. "Do you think I should go over there? You know, to give her some moral support?"

"I think we should just wait until we hear from her," Dylan said. Tera and her dad would probably be at it most of the night.

"You're right. Text me if you hear from her, and I'll do the same."

Dylan walked across the street to his house in a daze and up into his room. He couldn't imagine what Tera must be thinking. Or feeling. Her mom was alive. And it was Jessica! Was that even her real name? He wondered what she used to look like. She probably had dark hair like Tera. She definitely had the same green eyes. Mr. Paine had said she was a catalyst too. Dylan couldn't wait to hear what happened between Tera and her dad. He put his phone next to him just in case Tera needed him.

***

Dylan's phone buzzed right next to his ear. It was 8:00 am. Tera had texted.

COME OVER IN 15 MINUTES. BRING BOTH CRYSTALS.

Bring the crystals? Why? Dylan feared the worst. Had Tera struck a deal with her dad? She'd hand over the crystals in exchange for meeting her mom? Dylan's stomach roiled at the thought. But this was no time to argue with Tera. He'd do whatever she wanted if it meant she could see her mom.

The crystals still sat together in his Lego house. He didn't want them touching once he was around Tera in case she activated one, so he put them in two leather pouches he used to store rocks. Dylan threw on some clean clothes and dropped a pouch into each of his pants pockets, then headed downstairs. The house was quiet. His whole family must be sleeping in, so he tried to open the front door quietly.

When he stepped outside he stopped. The same green car that had been at Mr. Lyman's house was in Tera's driveway. Across the street, Kari and EJ both walked out of their houses. Dylan met them in the street.

"Did you guys get texts too?" he asked.

EJ and Kari nodded. "Dylan, do you have any idea what this is about?" Kari asked. "And whose car is that?"

"I don't know. But we're about to find out."

They walked up to Tera's house. She met them at the front door. Her eyes were red and puffy, and her hair was half up in a messy ponytail. Dylan guessed she hadn't slept all night.

"Are you okay?" Dylan whispered as he walked in. Tera gave a half smile and nodded.

She led them down the hall into the kitchen. Mr. Paine stood beside the table in the same clothes he had worn the night before. Sitting next to him was Jessica.

"Everyone, take a seat," Mr. Paine said, motioning to the kitchen chairs and folding chairs that had been added around the table. "All of you now know Jessica, Tera's mother." Jessica smiled.

Dylan glanced at Tera, who was looking down at her hands in her lap.

"After a long night of discussion, we have made a decision." Mr. Paine paused and looked at Jessica.

"Whoever it was at 4E that hired Frank to go after the earth crystal, isn't going to make another move unless he has something to go after," Jessica said. "We have to give him that something."

Dylan put his hands on his pockets. Nobody was getting the crystals. "I thought you were all about keeping the crystals and catalysts safe?" Dylan said, looking at Mr. Paine.

"I am. And we think the best way to do that now is to make sure each catalyst knows how to use their crystal to its fullest extent."

"I already know how," Kari said.

"Good." Jessica smiled. "I thought you might. That's why I gave you the other half of the wind crystal for your birthday."

Kari gasped. "That was *you*?"

"I found it by the creek after the tornado. You already had one half, so I thought you needed the other."

Kari smiled. "Wait until I show you what I can do. You should see what EJ can do too."

"Don't bring me into this!" EJ said. "I'm out."

"EJ, we need you to help with this," Tera said. "I'm just as scared as you to use my power."

"I'm not scared," EJ snapped.

"We can practice in a controlled environment, so nobody gets hurt," Jessica said. "I'll do it too. I've been waiting a long time to see what I can do as a catalyst, especially if Tera and I work together." Tera looked at her mom and gave a hint of a smile. Dylan wondered if they'd let him be part of the experiments even though he wasn't a catalyst. He would give anything to be there.

Mr. Paine sat down in a folding chair. "I know we're asking a lot of you kids, but if you can each master your power, then we can work together to draw out the individuals and put an end to this, so you won't have to worry anymore."

"That would be nice," Tera muttered.

"We'll help you," Jessica said. "We can all help each other. Dylan, did you bring the crystals?"

Dylan sank in his chair. He wasn't a catalyst. The only thing he was good for was giving up the crystals. Again. He reached into his pockets and tossed the pouches on the table.

Jessica reached for them. "Thank you. I know how protective you are of them."

"They're just rocks," he said under his breath. But that wasn't true. They were way more than just rocks.

"Dylan, we have a special job for you," Jessica said.

He crossed his arms, skeptical of what she'd say.

"There's still one more crystal out there," she said. "And we need to find it before someone else does. There's a good chance it's hidden in a cache too. You're the best geocacher we know. And with Mr. Lyman's help, we think you two can find it."

At the mention of Mr. Lyman, Dylan realized the green car in Mr. Lyman's driveway must have been Jessica's. They had probably already been talking about finding the water crystal. Dylan sat up straighter.

"I know I can do that," he said. "I'll geocache every single day if I have to until I find it."

"We'll help you with anything you need," Mr. Paine said. "The military has some pretty sophisticated tracking and GPS gear."

EJ groaned. "Oh great, now you'll never stop talking about your treasure hunting."

Dylan smiled. He knew he could find the last crystal. He wouldn't let his friends down. And it would be his greatest treasure yet.

the end.

About the Author

Kathy Sattem Rygg is the author of *The Crystal Cache* series as well as the author of the Hidden Gem award winning chapter books *Tall Tales with Mr. K* and *TALLER Tales with Mr. K*, and the author of the highly acclaimed middle grade book *Animal Andy*. She has more than 15 years of experience in marketing and public relations, and has held editorial positions for a number of publications. Ms. Rygg is from Omaha, NE, where she lives with her two children and enjoys sharing her love for writing.

About Knowonder

Knowonder is a leading publisher of engaging, daily content that drives literacy; the most important factor in a child's success.

Parents and educators use Knowonder tools and content to promote reading, creativity, and thinking skills in children from zero to thirteen.

Knowonder's products and books deliver original, compelling stories and content, creating an opportunity for parents to connect to their children in ways that significantly improve their children's success.

Ultimately, Knowonder's mission is to eradicate illiteracy and improve education success through content that is affordable, accessible, and effective.

www.knowonder.com

52021224R00116

Made in the USA
San Bernardino, CA
08 August 2017